KT-232-692

A

Renegade Gold

It was the end of the war. The South was beaten and her hopes and dreams shattered with the furling of the conquered 'stars and bars' of the Confederacy. But Travis Eade was still a man of the South, who clung to a will to live, who had the desire to carve a new life for himself and who yet had the courage to fight for survival.

Once a grey-clad rider with General Stonewall Jackson, Eade and a handful of former Confederate soldiers had been thrown by circumstance into the broiling wasteland of the Arizona desert. Fate brought the lovely Marguerite Norman into their midst, and now they were flung together in a wide-open, savage land menaced by the ruthless Apache Indians.

But the Apaches were not the only forces to be reckoned with and there were age old forces of lust and avarice at work within the white men themselves. Could Travis Eade stand against bloodthirsty Indians and the scheming treachery of men who had once been his comrades in battle, or would he meet the bloody fate of his beloved South?

Renegade Gold

MARTIN QUINN

A Black Horse Western

ROBERT HALE · LONDON

ISBN 0 7090 6936 7

Robert Hale Limited
Clerkenwell House
Clerkenwell Green
London EC1R 0HT

Typeset by
Derek Doyle & Associates, Liverpool.
Printed and bound in Great Britain by
Antony Rowe Limited, Wiltshire.

X000 000 029 5317

ONE

Up on the high ridge, the Apache lay with his near-naked body pressed tightly against the hot shale. He looked with slitted eyes through a gap in the scatter of sun-split rocks which studded the crest of the ridge.

He watched seven riders' down on the white-shimmering flats of the desert. Black Indian eyes followed their progress, a slow progress, for the seven rode weary horses which laboured under the pounding heat of the brassy gong of the sun. At the rear of the slowly moving file of horsemen, there rolled a wagon, pulled by a team of jaded horses. A species of rough canvas awning had been rigged up to cover most of the wagon and, from under it at the open tail of the wagon, there protruded the booted legs of a man lying in the lumbering vehicle.

The Apache thought his own thoughts. Seven men riding, an eighth driving the wagon and a ninth, either sick or dead, travelling as a passenger. He noted the glitter of sun smitten sidearms; the nondescript dress of the riders – not the blue uniforms of soldiers – and the direction in which they travelled. Then, he slithered backwards beyond the rim of the

5

ridge. In a matter of minutes, he was back in the camp of Quino and his renegade Apaches, hidden in the midst of rearing rock needles beyond the ridge.

Quino was waiting to hear what the lookout had to report. The renegade Indian leader was squat, ugly and scarred. His matted black hair hung below his shoulders and a greasy head-band held it out of his eyes. His breech-cloth contrasted with the upper garment he affected: the ragged, bleached remains of a blue cavalry tunic taken from the body of a trooper he had killed when he rode with Cochise in that chief's rampages of early 1861.

The lookout told his story with Indian economy of words and gestures. Nine white men were heading for the water-hole in the rock clusters north of here. It was news which brought a hard glitter to Quino's eyes and he began to grunt terse orders which sent lithe Apaches haring for picketed ponies.

Quino was more than half insane. His hatred of the whites was about equal to his hatred of his own people – Cochise's Chiricahua Apaches, who'd cast him out years before.

And nine men were down there on the flats . . . nine men to be butchered.

Nine white men.

Nine white men, Confederate soldiers in disguise, riding on a mission to save a cause which seemed to be lost. They wore tattered civilian clothing and broadbrimmed sombreros, crusted with the dust of mile after mile of sun-punished desert travel.

Major Travis Eade was their leader and he sat his tired animal at the fore of the slowly moving party, riding next to bulky Captain Clay Forrest. The rest of the party were cavalry non-coms: four sergeants

and three corporals, men chosen by high authority
in the Rebel army to undertake this hazardous
secret mission across the howling wilderness of the
Arizona deserts. Major Travis Eade was just twenty-
eight, the son of a Texas settler who had been among
the earliest to set foot in the big, empty land in pre-
Alamo days and who had named his first-born in
honour of the Alamo's commander. When only a
stripling, young Eade had travelled with his father
on Comanche-trading expeditions in Texas. Later, in
the middle-fifties, they'd scouted for the army in the
cactus-clawed, sun-hammered lands of New Mexico
and Arizona which came into United States' posses-
sion as part of the spoils of the war with Mexico of
1846.

It was because of his familiarity with this tangled
terrain that Major Travis Eade, Confederate cavalry
officer who had ridden with Stonewall Jackson, had
been placed in charge of the party which had travelled into Mexico and which was now returning
across the blazing wilderness to keep an imperative
date at a rendezvous over the Texas line. Eade was
tall and lean. His dark features were handsome, but
four years of war had stamped them with deep lines
of bitterness. A ragged scar slanted across his left
cheek, giving his mouth a perpetual quirk at one
corner. It was a relic of this war in which blue-clad
Federals met grey-garbed Rebels to battle out their
differences with cannon, muskets, bayonets and
sabres. It was a bullet-bite obtained in the autumn
of '62 when Lee and McClellan clashed at a hitherto
pleasant Maryland creek called Antietam and made
that name hideous.

Quino, now making ready to swoop upon the

wearily moving whites, had no conception of white men's methods of measuring time and the white men themselves would have required some moments of mental effort to arrive at an approximation of this day's date. It was just another blazing day of travel, one of a sequence of such days in which they seemed to ride outside time and space in this sun-tortured immensity of heat-hazed desert. Back in the more settled regions, where men had printed calendars to which they could refer, it was 29 April 1865.

These nine Southern soldiers in disguise had commenced their mission in mid-March, riding out of Texas for Sonora, Mexico. The South was then being beaten to its knees. Gone were the days of early victory when Beauregard's whooping Rebels sent the Yankees running in a panicky mob from the battlefield at Bull Run; when securely entrenched Confederates picked off the bluecoats as they tried to attack across an open field at Fredericksburg and when the Rebels gleefully sent a proud Yankee general who called himself 'Fighting Joe' Hooker running from a Virginia hamlet named Chancellorsville in a welter of rain, wind, mud and blood.

These, and other Confederate victories, had been gained before the fateful summer of 1863, the summer which brought the crippling defeats at Vicksburg and Gettysburg to the Confederacy. In mid-March, '65, the South fought gallantly and ferociously, but with the odds stacked hopelessly against it.

Yankee General Grant and his bluecoated horde pressed closer to Richmond every day, imperilling

the Confederate capital. Yankee General Sherman
and his plundering, burning 'bummers' had sliced
clear through Georgia like some Biblical plague sent
to punish the rebellious land, and Yankee General
Sheridan carried the torch of war down the
Shenandoah valley. The South, with its young men
gone, tried to fight back. Southern ranks were filled
with old men and young boys, many of them shoe-
less and all in rags.

Confederate economy was broken. All around the
Rebel coast, the heavily armed vessels of Lincoln's
navy held a ceaseless blockade. They had been there
since '61, ensuring that no cotton left the South to
bring in revenue from abroad and that no arms were
shipped into the Southern states. Penniless, the
Confederate States fought on, subsisting on meagre
rations and giving ground to the advancing Yankees
only grudgingly and then with high toll of life.

In mid-March. the South fought with dwindling
hope. Unrecognized by overseas nations though it
was, Jefferson Davis's rebel government still hoped
to steer the seceded states into a future in which
they would be an independent nation separated
from the United States.

It was in that month that the Confederacy sent
out Eade and his party in a belated and desperate
effort to replenish the Southern government's
coffers. Down in Mexico, there were forces working
for the Rebel cause, negotiating for the delivery of
gold bullion from south of the border into
Confederate hands. The scheme had been planned
over months during which Confederate spies and
couriers shuttled back and forth between Mexico
and Richmond, Virginia, negotiating the tangled

deserts of Arizona and New Mexico and the Rebel
state of Texas where a curious and almost private
war was going on between Lincoln's Federals and
Confederate guerillas.

The orders given to Eade and his party were plain
enough – they even sounded simple when considered as mere words: meet the party bringing the
gold from Mexico at a certain ruined mission in
Arizona and bring the bullion into Texas. There, it
was to be taken by another Rebel band through a
Confederacy split by Sherman's march, to Richmond
itself. Travis Eade did not know how they were
going to do it since, by mid-March, the greater part
of the once proud South swarmed with Northern
troops, but his assignment was the first part of the
project, not the second.

And that first part was bad enough. Down in New
Mexico and Arizona, there were strong sympathies
with the South, but these were mere territories, not
states, wild and wide open, filled with men who
owed allegiance to one side or the other, or simply to
their own personal selves. Then there were the
Apaches and the soldiers. Back in '61, on the very
eve of the Civil War. a US Army major by the name
of Bascom had arrested wily Cochise on a charge of
kidnapping a white boy. The Chiricahua chief had
escaped, gathered his bucks and set out on the
rampage, killing, plundering and burning in a
concentrated effort to drive the whites from Apache
lands. Then came the war and the Yankee soldiers
who had defended the desert garrisons against
Cochise and his kill-crazy war parties were with-
drawn to fight the Rebels and replaced by a volunteer outfit of tough Westerners known as the

California Column. They were Yankees under another name and the party of Confederates was faced with the task of moving secretly through a hostile terrain peopled by savage Apaches and blue-coated soldiers who took their orders from Washington. Through this wilderness, they had to move far from the sparse settlements and, on the return journey, they bore cases of bullion secreted in the lumbering wagon under sacks of provisions and cases of equipment, the trappings of the gold prospecting party the nine Confederates were supposed to be.

There were setbacks. On the south-bound journey, a vedette of California Column riders had stopped them in mid-Arizona. In an uneasy interview, the Southerners had bluffed it out with a scrubby bearded cavalry captain who, mercifully enough, seemed eager to return to his base at Fort McDowell as hastily as possible. He swallowed their prospecting story whole and took his vedette of bluebellies off over the parched land with a good-natured warning to the nine Rebels that if they were damn fools enough to go looking for gold out yonder they were welcome to it – and welcome to Cochise and his 'Pache varmints.

Two days after the meeting with the cavalrymen, they saw smoke spiralling up from the spiny ridges, shimmering in the heat hazes miles ahead. Apache signal fires!

Eade holed up the party in a cluster of high rocks. They stayed there three days and three nights. Tempers grew frayed in the enforced idleness. The water in their canteens dwindled and vanished. Each day, smoke-talk continued to float up from the far ridges to the south and answering puffs climbed

the flawless azure sky from a tiny line of buttes on
the hazy horizon. Cochise and his Chiricahuas plan-
ning more devilment, more than likely.

On the fourth day, there were no more smoke
signals. The Indians must have moved off. They
hadn't moved in the direction of the rocks where the
Confederate party lay or signs of their approach
would have been visible by sundown on that fourth
day. At sundown, Eade took his party out of the rock
cluster and they gingerly made southbound tracks:
the creaking cart, eight horses and nine dried-up
men who rode with tongues rattling in parched
mouths like pebbles in tin cans.

Through the night, they made a tortured progress
and the torture increased after sunup. The sun
seared their faces and hands, their tongues were
swollen and dry as sandpaper and their mounts
plodded mechanically onwards with drooping heads
for hour after hour.

Sometime in the mid-afternoon, they reached a
tinaja: a waterhole in mossy rocks, guarded by
saluting saguaro cactus.

They made fools of themselves. Every last man of
them.

Men and horses shoved their noses into the
brackish water together and drank noisily. They
would have kept at it until sundown if Eade and
Captain Clay Forrest had not roused their seven
men out of their half-crazed water orgy to pull back
the animals and tether them in the cactus clump
before they overdrank and distended their bellies.
They tied the horses, then got back to the water,
Eade and Forrest with them, sprawling in the rocks
and drinking more than their fill.

Presently, they tore themselves away and stretched in the scant shade of the cactus. Captain Clay Forrest, a Missouri man in his late thirties, bulkier than any Confederate had a right to be after four hard-scrabble years of war and with a thick-grown moustache which did little to hide a vicious mouth, fished in the pocket of his bleached shirt and produced a precious cigar stub. He lit it and smoked it with the elegance of a pre-war Virginia planter taking his ease.

They sprawled around the waterhole until close on sundown, occasionally venturing to the edge of the *tinaja* and taking a sip. At sundown, they filled their canteens, watered the horses again and struck out.

Two days later, they reached the rendezvous close to the border of the Mexican state of Sonora. The old Spanish mission, uninhabited for close on a century, crumbled in the sun with its bell tower empty and desert thorns clawing at its adobe walls. The place was deserted, save for a family of jackrabbits and a roadrunner which scooted out of the yawning door-way of the mission and hared for the tangled scrub and thorn with his neck a-bobbing eccentrically when he heard the riders approach. Something had happened to the Confederate contacts from over the border. They had not waited, but they had left abundant sign of their having been at the mission in the shape of horse-droppings and the butts of Mexican cigarillos.

Eade cursed the factors which had made them late for the rendezvous: the days of lying low in the rocks when they spotted the savages' signals; the hours wasted sprawling around the *tinaja*. Sergeant

Abner Mapes, prowling about the crumbled building
as the men stretched their legs and grumbled
steadily, spotted a pencilled message, scrawled close
to the mission door. He called Eade and Forrest.

'*Under the windows – inside*', they read. '*Can't
wait now, situation too dangerous. Even if you don't
make it here, it doesn't matter a damn now. Good
luck and to hell with the Union. Gribbon.*'

The Rebels gathered around in a bunch and
stared at the message on the mission wall. Gribbon
was an undercover Confederate working south of
the border and it was he who was to meet them with
a party – and the bullion – from Mexico. The
message made as much sense as the loose tongued
talk of a drunk or a man turned crazy with the sun.
Eade's party repeated it time and again '. . . *dangerous situation . . .*' they murmured '. . . *doesn't matter
a damn now . . .*' they murmured.

But the bit about '. . . *under the window –
inside . . .*' made sense enough when they took their
prospecting shovels from the wagon and dug in
recently turned earth beneath the gaping aperture
of the single window inside the old Spanish building. The bullion was there – a dozen iron-bound
cases of it. They unearthed the cases, opened some
and gazed on row upon row of glittering ingots, sufficient in number to make staid old President 'One-
eyed Jeff' Davis of the Confederate States of
America jump with joy.

It was on the day following the discovery of the
cryptic message and the cached bullion, the first day
of the return journey, that the party of disguised
secessionist soldiers hit trouble in spades. The small
wagon, now heavily laden with the bullion cases

stowed carefully under the heaps of provisions and mining gear, slithered on unsafe ground at the edge of a deep desert declivity. Rocks bedded in loose, dry shale gave way under the weight of the lumbering vehicle and the wagon pitched with one wheel in the declivity and the other three turning fruitlessly against dusty shale.

There was a frenzied dismounting and a sweating, swearing, fifteen minutes of shoving and hauling at the heavy vehicle to shift it up the powdery edge of the declivity and re-establish it on four wheels on solid ground. They almost had the chore completed when more earth crumbled and the wagon rolled back swiftly with a wrenching grind of axles. The men who shoved it from the back went leaping clear of its path, moving under reflex actions.

But one was too late. Corporal Dan Clyman, a 21-year-old youngster from Texas. was swiped by the backward spinning wheel, rolling downward in a cloud of dust.

Clyman went pitching back with the wheel, then he was under it, yelling hoarsely as it rolled over his left shoulder, the weight of the bullion forcing him down into the soft, hot shale.

Eade, Forrest and Clyman's companions went to the back of the wagon in a knot of gasping, snorting energy, striving to shove the wheel off the sobbing man pinned under it. Clyman had fainted by the time they hauled him out from under the wagon.

His shoulder was crushed, his collar bone was certainly broken and Eade had a doubt about his upper arm. That seemed to be broken, too; but, if there was a mercy to be thankful for in such a situation, it was that there was no sign of an exposed

bone. A compound fracture would take gangrene all
too easily, but there was a chance that Clyman's
shoulder and arm could be splinted up reasonably
well until they managed to get him to a surgeon.

'Fort McDowell, that's the nearest place we're
likely to find a surgeon,' commented Eade, survey-
ing Clyman's unconscious form after he and Forrest
had trussed his shoulder and arm in makeshift
splints and made him as comfortable as possible on
a rough bed atop the hidden bullion cases in the
wagon.

'Fort McDowell!' exploded Forrest. 'A Yankee fort
full of them bluebellies from California – we can't go
there with this wagon. Suppose those California
Column Yankees discover the bullion; maybe we
should strike for Prescott, but not a damyank fort!'

Major Travis Eade shook his head slowly.
Prescott, named only the previous year as capital of
Arizona Territory, was a settlement in which the
party of Confederates might pass with ease in
search of a doctor, but it was several days' journey
north of this point. Fort McDowell, up in the Gila
River country, was far enough away, but it was the
nearest location where a surgeon would be found.

'It'll have to be McDowell,' Eade contended. 'We'll
have to bluff it out – cache the wagon on the desert,
or something – but we must get Clyman to a doctor
as quickly as possible.'

Captain Clay Forrest blew out his sun-seared
cheeks, his dark eyes registering exasperation and
almost contempt as a reaction to Eade's suggestion.
Eade didn't much care for Forrest. Before the war,
when Frank Pierce was President of the United
States and a ceaseless turmoil raged between

Missouri and Kansas, Forrest had been a Missouri 'Border Ruffian'. He had been one of the army of pro-slavery Missouri men who had marched over the border into Kansas to terrorize the town of Lawrence on the day in 1855 when Kansans went to the poll to decide whether Kansas would hold negroes to be free men or chattels.

As a Confederate, Forrest had proved himself a good officer, but he had a streak of middle-border brutality which Eade didn't like and it was beginning to show itself now.

'Seems we're takin' a big risk for the sake of this youngster,' he growled. 'Can't see why we should go pushin' ourselves into Fort McDowell on his account. He could rest easy enough as he is until we make it to Texas.'

'Rest easy be damned!' snorted Travis Eade. 'He's unconscious now, but when he comes to his senses, that shoulder will give him hell. He needs skilled attention – and quick. Quit backbitin', Captain, remember I'm in command of this mission.'

In a hanging moment of tension, the officers were aware that the men were standing around them, silently watching this brief, but telling, flaring of tempers. Eade was aware, too, of something that smacked of outright contempt in Forrest's eyes. It was almost as though the big Missouri man was saying: 'To hell with you and your command!' without using his lips to convey the message.

Forrest continued to push the argument.

'Those bluebellies at the fort will want to know how Clyman was hurt. If we tell them he was run over by the wagon, they'll want to know what's in the wagon to make it so heavy.'

'That's one of the risks we'll have to take. I want that boy to have proper attention,' Eade retorted. 'We're going to the fort and that's the finish of it!'

Forrest shrugged his shoulders. 'Fort McDowell it is, then, so long as you give the orders!' There was a distinct note of scorn in his voice, but Travis Eade let it ride. He glimpsed the faces of the men as they prepared to mount up once more. Dark-burned, rebel-lean faces under the shading brims of broad hats, they all had a certain hardness and inscrutability. Sergeant Abner Mapes, Sergeant Ben Forman, Sergeant Israel Janniver, Sergeant Gustave Dufay, Corporal Charlie Tucker, Corporal Dick Grover and Corporal George Wain. They were shrewd and knowing men, cut from the clay of the South and shaped and hardened in battle. There was little these men had to learn – and little of what they already knew was given away in their faces. Nevertheless, Travis Eade felt that they were as much aware as he was that the anger they had seen sparking between the two officers could be irritated by time into a harshly grinding grudge.

They mounted and rode. They moved slowly across the parched land. There was little conversation and the riding became the mechanical, sun-pounded progress they had followed for day after day.

Hours passed and the party crawled across the vast floor of the desert. Blue haze shimmered on the far horizon and it was against the mistiness of the purpled distances that a thin, dark banner of what at first appeared too be smoke was caught by Eade's wilderness-trained eyes.

Silently, he considered the distantly spiralling

stream. It was not Indian fire-smoke. It was the dust
of either a party of riders or some sort of vehicle far
ahead of them, moving fairly quickly and almost at
right-angles to their own line of travel. Eade seemed
to be alone in sighting it and he watched it for fully
ten minutes before drawing Captain Clay Forrest's
attention to it.

'We're not the only travellers out today. Look
ahead,' he commented. Forrest followed the major's
pointing finger and discerned the far away smudge
of risen, moving dust.

'Apache war party, do you think?' he asked.

'Can't say. It isn't moving towards us, but it is
coming up to our path on an angle. Could be we'll
meet up in an hour or so.'

The party of Rebels kept the scarf of rising dust in
sight for almost an hour, then they lost it as they
rode into a sweep of arid land dominated on either
side by high-rearing crests of rock. Here, the tower-
ing rim-rock cast shadows across the alkali-
whitened floor of the desert, which offered some
relief from the hammering heat of the sun as the
riders and their wagon moved through them.

Ahead, the rim-rock on either side became scattered and broken islands, finally petering away to
leave the desert wide open before the slowly moving
party. They were deep in the tract of land guarded
by the high crests and a long way from attaining the
open width of the shimmering desert when Travis
Eade saw something with the corner of his eye
which chilled him as though icy water had been
pitched over him.

Against a sun-splashed rock, high above his head
and over to his right, he saw an immobile Indian.

His eyes slithered quickly from side to side, but he did not turn his head. There was another Apache, also holding a motionless pose, a little below the first and, over to the left, there were at least three sets of breech-clouts and head-bands squatting in the high rocks and almost blending with the fretted shards of sun-split natural sculpture.

'Don't move your head,' Eade whispered to Forrest. 'There are Apaches watching us. They're on either side of us. They've got us holed up.'

Forrest's dark eyes darted from side to side under the shading brim of his hat. Apaches were multiplying in the high rocks, coming into being suddenly as though spontaneously created by the rocks themselves and standing or squatting motionless as though part of the rocks.

' *'Paches in the rocks!*' hissed Eade urgently. '*Pass it down the line and don't grab for your irons until I give the order. Then, cluster around the wagon and ride like blazes out of this place!*'

The urgent order crisped down the straggle of slowmoving riders. There was an almost imperceptible bunching in of riders towards the wagon and, in the rearing rocks flanking the party, Apaches thickened. Where there had been eight, there were now sixteen – all silent, immobile, waiting the order to attack.

And the opening of this death trap lay several yards ahead. Only the wildest of mad dashes could take the party of whites, with its lumbering wagon and injured man, out of the ambush, but that was the move Travis Eade had determined upon.

The party of Confederates waited with tensed nerves, striving to conceal from the watching savages that they knew of their presence. They waited, horses plodding laboriously under the fierce sun, sweat sliding in icy runnels from under their hat brims, hands itching to grab for holstered Navy Colts or to unsling Spencer carbines, but not yet daring until the order was given. . . .

And the opening of this tangled place of ambush lay yards ahead. Too far, it seemed, for a successful dash out of the Apache-swarmed rims. Hearts pounded, mouths were dry, sweat clammed itching trigger fingers, patient hoofs plodded slowly, slowly, slowly. . . .

'*Now!*' yelled Travis Eade. He raked his horse with his spurs, clawed for his Colt and voiced the first note of the eerie, drawn-out 'Rebel yell'. His companions took it up, screeching fit to split their lungs, as Confederate soldiers had screeched that nerve-tearing cry of defiance in Virginia, Maryland and Pennsylvania when pitching themselves against the tides of blue marching under the stars and stripes. The wagon, with its injured passenger bouncing cruelly, rumbled over hard-packed alkali dust with iron rimmed wheels striking sparks from occasional rocks as Corporal Dick Grover, hunched over the rumps of the team, whipped the animals to a panicky lick. The horsemen bunched close about the wagon, their mounts stretched flat out. Navy Colts were glittering in the sun, Spencer carbines were cleared of saddle scabbards and the madly riding bunch of whites slammed random shots back at the Apaches who were now sending arrows whining down from the rock crests.

The savages were late with their offensive. Just as the eerie Rebel yell had so often scared Union

troops, the blood curdling screech, voiced at the
moment Major Travis Eade and his party started
their desperate run out of the rock guarded ambush
spot, took the Apaches by surprise. White men who
screamed like demons were something entirely new
in their experience. For a moment, the yelling horsemen had set Quino and his desert warriors back on
their heels by making their furious dash for the
open wilderness just when the Indians imagined
they were securely in the trap.

But the advantage was short-lived. The Apaches
had stirred themselves out of their shocked moment
under the yelling of the fanatic Quino. Now, they
were sending arrows whistling down from their
stations in the rims. Bouncing in his saddle in an
eye-stinging chaos of hoof risen dust and swirling
smoke from the weapons of his companions which
were loosing shots back at the attacking Indians,
Travis Eade got off two shots with his Colt. With a
deep satisfaction, he watched two savages pitch
down from the rocks as his shots hit them. He was
aware of Captain Clay Forrest riding close to him,
twisted about in his saddle and blazing his Colt at
the attacking Apaches. Through the blur of dust and
smoke, he saw Apaches swarming along the rock
ridges with an indefinable grandeur, half naked
figures with hair streaming and lithe bodies slithering sure-footedly over the gnarled rocks. Lances
were pitched down upon the madly hastening travellers and the fletches of arrows made harsh whis-
perings on the desert air.

An arrow thumped into the dry wood of the
crazily lumbering wagon. Eade saw Sergeant
Gustave Dufay, a wiry Louisiana Creole, take an

arrow through the heart as he was canted about in bucking saddle leather, drawing a bead on one of the Indians with his carbine. Dufay slithered limply down to the ground, his mount with its neck stretched out and nostrils flaring, running riderless in the knot of thundering riders.

Forrest made a desperate attempt to haul his horse about.

'I'm goin' back after Dufay!' he yelled to Eade.

'It's too late – he's dead!' Eade bawled. 'Keep riding. If you turn back, you'll get yourself killed!'

A whining arrow skimmed Forrest's head and he gave his attention to triggering vindictive shots up at the Apaches, continuing to ride in the furiously pounding mass of bobbing horses and men clustered about the wagon. The brief, madcap gesture was typical of Forrest, thought Eade. Forrest had a quarrelsome and stubborn streak, but he was all soldier. Turning back for an injured comrade was part of his code and he would have made a dash back to Dufay almost instinctively if Eade had not restrained him.

Now, the hastening party was drawing close to the opening of the walled-in tract of desert and it had burst through the thickest concentration of high-positioned Apaches. The wilderness flattened before them, but a new hazard was gathering on their tails.

Quino had sent mounted warriors streaking and yelling after the whites when he realized that his attempt to jump them in the rock-guarded terrain had failed. Riding like demons on wiry mustangs, the braves came hard in the wake of the retreating whites.

Eade, his Navy Colt exhausted of ammunition, was crouched over the pommel of his saddle, pumping a round into the breech of his Spencer.

'Forrest, stick with the wagon!' he bellowed through the choking dust. 'Janniver and Forman, fall back with me and pick some of those devils off!'

Janniver and Forman, doughty fighting men and good marksmen, obeyed, slackening the speed of their animals to join Eade at the rear of the fleeing party and turning in their saddle to face the pursuing desert warriors. The wagon and its escort of dust-rising riders rumbled ahead in a white haze of swirling alkali. The Apaches, flattened on their mustangs, were coming hard. Eade and his rearguard companions lost speed deliberately, their bodies twisted around in their jerking saddles, Spencers raised to their shoulders.

'Take one each – and don't miss!' bellowed Eade.

The combined reports of three Spencers ripped out over the thunder of hoofs and the cacophany of Indian shrieks. Two Apaches slumped down from the bare backs of their baring mustangs. The mount of a third, mortally wounded, crumpled abruptly and rolled on its kicking rider before he could slither clear.

'Three more!' rasped Eade at the top of his voice. They took three more and the Apaches, with their ardour now considerably dampened, slackened speed, bunched themselves tighter – but they still rode in pursuit.

'Catch up with the others,' ordered Eade and the trio set its horses thundering for the main party.

Up ahead, there was a ragged straggle of rocks and saguaro cactus. It looked a likely place in which

to hole up and finish this fight from an entrenched
position. There was something else.

Heading for the rocks, almost at right angles to
the line of travel of the party of racing Southerners,
there was a Concord coach and team – and with the
team rode an escort of soldiers. The bright sun
sheened saddle trappings, sabres and carbines. It
glinted off brass and showed Yankee blue in the
swirling dust risen by the coach, team and escort.
The coach looked civilian enough, but the soldiery
riding alongside it was undoubtedly men of the
California Column, which guarded these Apache-
infested regions while the regular United States
troops were away at the war.

This, then was the cause of the banner of risen
dust which Eade's party had spotted long before,
away in the vast vacancy of the desert: an escorted
passenger coach, probably heading for Fort
McDowell and, perhaps, *en route* for Prescott. Like
the company of disguised Southern soldiers, the
driver and his guard of soldiers had notions of
holing up in the rock pile and making a stand. Even
as the party which escorted the bouncing wagon
with its load of bullion and injured passenger
neared the rocks with mounted Indians close behind
and more streaming on stretched-out ponies from
the gully in which the Apaches had attempted their
ambush, the party of bluecoats riding with the coach
slammed a spatter of shots towards the Indians.
Gradually, with savage yells sounding loud behind
them, Eade and his men reached the rocks. From its
own angle of approach, the escorted coach drew
nearer, driver, guard and soldiers obviously resolved
to make common cause with the hounded whites

about to hole up and fight off the Apaches who were now multiplying across the desert floor like a locust swarm issuing from the rock guarded gully. They were coming on ponies and coming fast. Quino, who had seen the whites and their wagon slither out of the ambush all too easily, was urging his braves to make a swift killing and sending almost every one of his renegade followers after the whites.

There was an opening in the scattering of rocks and boulders sufficiently wide for the wagon to pass through. Three of Eade's party manhandled it through while Eade, Forrest and the rest pitched themselves down among the scorched rocks, blasting with Spencers and picking off Apaches. They halted the Indian charge for a moment, causing the savages to whirl about and ride back out of range, then they scooted for the deep cover of the rocks into which the wagon had gone. The place was a dried up water hole where rocks were piled high around a sandy basin, grown about with cactus. It was a natural strong-point which might be held indefinitely against enemies who attacked across the open wilderness between this point and the gully where Quino's Apaches had attempted their ambush. Might be held indefinitely, that is, if there was food and water to sustain the defenders.

Eade, Forrest and the remainder of the party, panting and sweating, slithered down among the rocks, the wagon with Clyman inside it having been halted close to the edge of the dried-up basin. From outside the cactus-guarded rock cluster, there came the yipping and shrieking of the Apaches as they mustered in a great cloud of dust out on the floor of the desert, well out of carbine range. Nearer, there was a thump of hoofs, the clink of trappings and the rumbling and creaking of the coach as it drew close to the rocks in which the Confederates were sprawled gripping their carbines and Colts. The bluecoated escort soldiers could be heard yelling and swearing at the cluster of Apaches and they loosed off sporadic shots as though to ensure that the desert warriors kept their distance.

Major Travis Eade slithered among sun-split boulders and saluting saguaro cactus until he reached a position from which he could see the approaching company of whites. He lay in hot shale and looked down at the halted coach at the bottom of a gentle slope of ground which slanted from the rock cluster to the ill-defined trail the coach and soldiers had been following.

The California Column cavalry men – there were only six of them – had dismounted along the rise and they were squatting beside their standing horses with carbines ready, making a guard for the civilian driver and coach guard who were taking the team of four out of the Concord's shafts and making to walk the animals up the slope to the protective rocks.

As he watched the two men frenziedly yanking the horses from between the shafts, Eade saw the door of the coach open and a solitary passenger came out of the vehicle to hurry up the slope towards the natural strong-point which housed Eade and his party.

Major Travis Eade scratched his grizzled chin in an unconscious fashion as he pondered upon the perversity of fate. It was bad enough that there were kill-crazy Apaches swarming across the landscape;

bad enough that they, a Southern party on a secret mission, were going to be holed up with blue-bellied Yankees while they had a secret load of bullion and a wounded man on their hands, but, to complicate matters, the one and only passenger the coach had carried was a girl!

And, as she came scurrying up the slope to where he sprawled, holding her skirts and struggling with a travelling bag, but making good speed for all that, Eade saw that the girl was about twenty-two and just about the prettiest he'd ever seen.

TWO

A breath of hot wind moved through the rock cluster, bringing the ominous yells of Quino's Apaches, mustering for an attack out on the floor of the desert. Eade's party had secured the team and the wagon in which the semi-conscious Clyman lay in the arid declivity that once was a water-hole. They had positioned themselves behind rocks, cradling Spencers and gripping Colts, looking down upon the bunching Apaches.

Travis Eade ordered hastily: 'We're going to share this hole with these bluebellies. Remember our story – we're prospectors. Don't any of you use military titles to each other!' Then, he rose from the place where he squatted, moved part way down the slope to meet the girl from the coach and tipped his battered hat to her as they drew nigh each other.

'Allow me to carry your bag, Ma'am,' Eade offered.

She was, Eade thought again, about the prettiest girl he had ever seen. She had been hastening up the drift of shale and the exertion had brought a touch of high colour to her soft cheeks. Her large eyes were bright. Ringlets of dark, lustrous, hair escaped from the bonnet which framed her face, a

face which smiled at the tall, tattered, skin-black-
ened and dust-peppered apparition who confronted
her.

'You're very kind,' she responded demurely.

Yankee, thought Travis Eade. *She talks like a
Yankee. She sure has courage. This is no place for a
woman, but she's smiling.*

He assisted the girl up the remainder of the slope.
The coach driver and guard came in their wake,
prodding the fractious, jumpy team up the slope,
and the six blue-clad cavalrymen came hastening
behind them.

Men, woman and horses scrambled into the circle
of rocks guarding the once lush water hole. The
senior of the six California Column soldiers was a
middle-aged sergeant with a spiky beard and long-
horn moustaches. He nodded to Eade as casually as
though they were a couple of cronies meeting on a
familiar street.

'Figured I'd have my party hole up here with you
when I saw you were heading for this spot,' he
commented, gruffly. 'If the varmints had turned
their attentions to us – which they would have done
as soon as they got some satisfaction out of you –
they'd have treated us the way that coach out of
Prescott was treated a couple of weeks back. Luckily,
you outran 'em, so I figured we'd take an option on
making a fight of it along with you. That's a sight
better than us and the horses being butchered
plumb easy. Then, we got the young woman to think
of. My name's Haggerty, from the garrison at Fort
McDowell. That two-striper over there is my second
in command, Corporal Hertz. Pretty good fellow,
Hertz, but if he suggests a game of cards, don't have

any truck with him. Not that we're likely to have time for a game if what I think is buildin' up out there comes down on us.' The sergeant jerked his forage-capped head in the direction of the desert beyond the protecting rocks.

Travis Eade liked the man at first sight. He liked his gruff, matter-of-fact, manner of speaking, too. Sergeant Haggerty might wear the blue shirt of the Union, but he had a certain inspiring aplomb. He possessed the wisdom of a veteran and the shrewdness of one who knew a good – or bad – thing when he saw one. Right now, he was seeing a bad thing, but he was not making any bones about it.

They squatted together on a flat rock, Eade replenishing the magazine of his Spencer, the cavalry sergeant nursing his own well-maintained carbine. Around them, Eade's men, the cavalry corporal, the four troopers and the driver and guard were lying on their stomachs squinting through the apertures between the rocks at the menacing Apaches. They accepted each other with a lack of formality. They were white men about to stand off Apaches and it was not the time or place to ask after a man's name, his place of origin or his destination.

The girl made a lonely little figure, sitting apart from the men close to the rim of the shale-filled hollow which had held water once, but which might have been dry even before the Spaniards ventured to this region three centuries before.

Out beyond the rocks, Quino's Apaches were keeping up a frenzied yipping, obviously a scare tactic aimed at the whites forted up in the rocks.

Travis Eade broached a subject which had raised

curiosity in him the moment the sergeant had mentioned it.

'What happened to the coach out of Prescott a couple a weeks back?' he wanted to know.

Haggerty looked at him curiously. 'Massacred,' he said flatly. 'Everybody riding in it and even the horses – just butchered. I thought everybody this side of the Mexican line knew about it. It was Quino – the same varmint that's out yonder whooping up his braves. Cochise is bad enough, but Quino is just plumb crazy. Even Cochise has disowned him!' The sergeant fished in the pocket of his greasy tunic and produced a half-smoked cigar. He pushed it into his mouth but did not light it. 'What're you fellows doing out here?' he asked.

'Prospecting,' Eade said. 'We've been grubbing in the desert for weeks past.'

Haggerty grinned. 'Thought you'd make an early start with spring, eh? Suppose you found more trouble than good luck. I did some grubbing after gold myself once. That's what took me to California in the first place. Come from Pennsylvania originally, but I went off west with the rush of '49. Never did find gold, but I settled in California. On the whole, I'm glad I went.' He fell silent for a minute then added with a rueful edge to his voice, 'On the other hand, if I hadn't gone to California, I wouldn't be in this outfit and if I wasn't in this outfit I wouldn't be in this fix now.' He spat into the shale and sat chewing the cold cigar in a reflective fashion.

Eade joined the men sprawled in the rocks watching the Apaches on the desert. He lay beside Clay Forrest and squinted through a gap between two rocks. There was a churning of dust on the desert floor where knots of mounted Indians were moving restlessly around.

'They're fixing something,' grunted Eade. 'Probably aim to rush at us in one mighty charge.'

'Sure. They won't be outdone,' answered Forrest. 'We slipped them once but that'll only give the varmints more determination to finish us off. What's that Yankee sergeant been talkin' about? He ask any awkward questions?'

'No. He seems all calm and collected and ready to fight and not much concerned about anything but those 'Paches.'

Captain Clay Forrest made a noncommittal sound in his throat and turned his attention to the distant Indians once more.

Behind them, the girl's voice enquired brusquely: 'Who has any water?'

Eade and Forrest turned their heads. She was behind them, squatting so that her bonnet and light blue crinoline dress did not show over the barrier of rocks between the water-sink and the Indians. Her presence was a sudden sobering factor among men who had been lying with tensed nerves and imaginations running riot on the theme of the over-whelming odds facing them. From their various positions in the rocks, they turned to face the girl. Most of them had forgotten about her. Eade saw their eyes considering her. There were Mapes, Janniver, Forman, Tucker, Wain and Grover of the Confederate party; there were the four California Column troopers, their corporal and sergeant and there were the two leathery civilians of indeterminate age, the driver and guard of the coach.

'Well?' demanded the girl. 'Who has a canteen

with water in it? There's a man down there who needs a drink.' She jerked her head back towards the floor of the waterhole where the wagon containing the injured Clyman stood among the tightly bunched, tethered horses. Captain Clay Forrest nudged Eade's leg violently with his bunched fist. In the fury of the past few minutes, they had forgotten about Clyman and the bullion, but the girl had discovered the injured corporal and it looked as though the unwelcome attention of the Yankee sergeant and his soldiers might be focused on the wagon with its hidden bullion.

'There's plenty in my canteen, ma'am,' said a bluecoat, a youth whose lack of years was not disguised by the moustache he was trying to cultivate. 'It's on my horse. Mine's the black with the white blaze on his head.'

'Thank you,' responded the girl. She turned to Eade. 'What happened to the man in the wagon?' she wanted to know.

'He was hurt in an accident. The wagon went over him.'

'He's rambling and he needs a drink,' she said almost curtly. She turned and, with a natural dignity hard to define, made her way down the sloping sides of the dried-out sink to the horses.

There came a sporadic yipping from out on the desert. The defenders of the rock-cluster moved closer to the natural barricade, sprawling in the dry, sun-beaten shale. Through the breaks in the scatter of rocks and cactus, they saw the Apaches whirling in a dust-hazed cluster of horses, fanning out into a long line of mustangs, preparing to make a charge. Then, they were advancing at a furious rush, riding for the rock studded water sink on a broad front with a constant high pitched screaming.

The cavalry sergeant slithered into a position between Eade and Forrest. He yanked his forage cap over his eyes, laid his Spencer carbine on a rock and, as if he had all the time in the world, fished a clumsy flint-and-wheel lighter from his tunic pocket and touched a light to his cigar. By the time he picked up his carbine again, the charging Apaches were within range.

THREE

A ragged blaze of firing greeted the Apaches as they neared the rocks. Several Indians squirmed from the backs of their mustangs, but the charge continued to thunder ahead with the hammer of unshod hoofs backed by the shrieking of the savages.

Major Travis Eade lay against a heat-split rock with his carbine hot in his hands. He was aware of the slam of Clay Forrest's carbine at his left and the pungent whiff of Sergeant Haggerty's cigar spicing the stink of cordite smoke from his right. It must be damned bad tobacco to smell so strongly above the powder, thought Eade absently – as he pumped another round into the Spencer.

The Apaches were moving in towards the rock-cluster with an odd illusion of slowness and a savage majesty to the way in which they clung to the backs of their unsaddled mustangs with jet black, greased hair streaming in the wind. Arrows and hurled lances began to strike among the rocks. Eade and his companions blasted their carbines and revolvers at the advancing front of mounted attackers.

Then, the world split into a dusty, din-shattered mosaic which Travis remembered afterwards in a

series of independent mental pictures just as he
remembered the battles of Antietam and Gettysburg
and other clashes of the blue and grey.

One segment of the advancing line of pony-kick-
ing Apaches was checked by the ragged fusillade of
shots from the defenders of the water sink; but a
hard-riding knot of yelling braves came thundering
forward, forming into a determined spearhead as
stricken Apaches hit the ground and others tried to
angle their mounts away from the threat of a second
such head-on volley. The determined ones were
coming in at a furious lick. In a crazy succession of
then-now, Eade remembered firing another blast
with his Spencer, then the Apaches were afoot,
swarming up the rocks to the entrenched whites.
Some of the warriors were dead or wounded at the
base of the rocks which guarded the desert *tinaja*,
but others were clambering over the rock wall
manned by Eade's men and the California Column
soldiers.

Eade was in the thick of them. Like a man awakening from a deep slumber to be faced with harsh
reality, he found that he was standing in a smoke-
hazed tableau in which he lashed out with a clubbed
carbine at painted faces and greasy headbands. The
rocks were filled with the blast of weapons, the
shrieks of Apaches and the hoarse swearing of
whites. Something hit Eade across the jaw and he
went spinning against a rock, telling himself, even
though preoccupied with the salt taste of blood in
his mouth, that he must hang on to his carbine.

Fingers grabbed at his throat. He saw an
Apache's painted face grimacing into his own and he
felt curiously weak and wearied. The savage was

strangling him and he was too dulled to fight back.

Then, the tightening grip at his throat was relaxed abruptly. Eade opened his eyes and saw that Sergeant Haggerty was hauling the Apache off him, yanking him back by a handful of his long, black hair. Fighting for his breath, Eade watched Haggerty clap the mouth of his Colt behind the savage's ear and shoot him through the skull. Then, Eade was in the midst of the tumbling bodies again, swinging the clubbed carbine with all his might.

Out of the corner of his eye, he saw figures moving in the smoke beyond the tiny segment of the fight where he was occupied. They seemed to be ghost figures, living in a world detached from that in which he clubbed at swarming Apaches. He saw a bluecoated cavalryman go stumbling blindly by. It was not until the soldier fell on his face and lay still that Eade realized he had an arrow in his back. He saw a figure in tattered civilian clothing draped over one of the rocks: one of his party, Janniver, he thought absently, or was it Mapes? He saw the girl, looking like a wraith in her light crinoline dress and poke bonnet, emerge out of the swirling powder-smoke and dust and shoot an Indian through the chest with a tiny Derringer pistol as he made a grab for her.

There was something in seeing her that spurred Eade on. In a crazed moment in which blood pounded at his temples and tears of rage blurred his sight, he whooped out a rasping Rebel yell. He was clubbing madly, whirling the carbine in a fury which consumed every fibre of his being and bawling the names of his men, yelling for them to rally to him.

Abruptly, the fight was over and Eade was stag-

gering through a tangle of bodies and rocks, panting
for breath and with blood streaming from his cut
mouth. It took him a full minute to realize that
Quino's Apaches were in retreat. They had scrambled out of the rocks, leaving their dead, and a
mounted mass of Indians was hazing for the rock
gully in which they had jumped Eade's party.

Clay Forrest and a knot of defenders were sprawling in the rocks at the edge of the cluster, pegging
parting shots after the retreating Indians.

'They've decided this is not their day for a fight,'
commented Sergeant Haggerty as Travis Eade
seated himself on a rock to regain his breath.
'They've taken off to dance a little and listen to their
witch-doctors. They'll be back when the signs are
right. Meantime, they'll probably keep us pinned
down in this darned sink. That was quite a fight you
put up, Mister.'

'How many have we lost?' Eade wanted to know.

'A couple of your friends and three of my men.
Two or three more of us got cuts and bruises. We did
almighty well considering the number of them
varmints that got in here.' The sergeant spoke with
an almost boisterous attitude. Then he deflated his
own high spirited enthusiasm. 'They'll be back.' he
warned. 'Quino has no intention of letting us sneak
out of here. Every movement we make will be
watched from those rims yonder.'

Travis Eade came to his feet and made a gloomy
survey of the water sink. Dead Indians, most killed
by shots fired from the whites' guns at devastatingly
close range, lay tangled in the dust and rocks. With
them were three of the Fort McDowell troopers –
and among the dead was Corporal Dick Grover

while Sergeant Israel Janniver was draped in death over the rocks which separated the party of whites from the Apaches now holed up in the far rim-rocks.

Eade spat blood into the dust in a spontaneous act of disgust and frustration.

What a way for it to end, he thought. The mission had gone so well so far. Then, in a matter of hours, Clyman was injured, Dufay, Grover and Janniver were dead. And they were pinned down in this dried-out water-hole, under the eye of crazy Quino and his Apaches. There was little doubt that it would be a mere matter of time before they all went the way of Dufay, Grover, Janniver, the dead blue-coats and the people whose butchered bodies had been found by the ambushed coach out of Prescott a couple of weeks before – victims of Quino, all of them.

Sergeant Haggerty, sucking the now spent butt of his cigar, moved away to assist one of the California Column troopers who was trying to bandage an arrow-slashed arm with a piece torn from his tunic and Captain Clay Forrest sat wearily beside Eade.

'It's lookin' bad,' he rumbled. 'These damn' 'Paches got us dead to rights an' I don't see us gettin' clear of here with our souls an' bodies stuck together.' He rubbed his thick moustache with the back of his hand. 'Then there's all that gold in the wagon down on the bed of the sink. All that darned gold!'

'We'll get out some damned way,' Travis Eade grunted, trying to fill his voice with a conviction he did not feel. 'We've got to. A lot depends on our getting that gold into Texas, then into Richmond.'

'Yeah,' Forrest said hollowly.

The girl came up from the bottom of the water

sink. She had been at the wagon and she held the
big military canteen belonging to the young soldier
with the wispy moustache. Powdersmoke had blackened her face and unruly strands of dark hair fell
from under her bonnet. She somehow managed to
retain her air of calm dignity and it was hard to see
her as the woman who had stood in the thick of a
fight not ten minutes before, triggering a Derringer
into the chest of an Apache.

She jerked her head towards the wagon on the
dusty floor of the once rich water-hole.

'Your friend down there is sleeping,' she informed
them gravely. 'I went to give him a drink but found
him asleep so I decided to let him rest. He's been out
of his mind with pain and raving. I stayed down
there through most of the fight with my little pistol
ready. I didn't want those savages to find him and
kill him. It was only when I realized how many of
them were over the rocks and fighting up here that
I decided it was time I came up and did some shooting.'

'You did fine – fine,' praised Eade. He admired the
girl for her outright courage and, somehow, she
shamed him. It was the knowledge that she had
stood by Clyman through most of the fight that
humbled him. In the tumbling fury of the battle, he
had forgotten about the injured corporal lying atop
the hidden bullion cases. Womanlike, this slight girl
had stayed down there with him to defend him
against the savage attackers. She had the cool,
courageous quality that made some women great, he
thought, like that Englishwoman, Miss Nightingale,
or the nursing woman the Yankees were so proud of,
what was her name, Clara Barton? All in all, Eade

reflected, this bunch of men, ill-assorted and thrust into the teeth of death by fickle circumstance, could be mighty grateful that the lone woman among them was one of high calibre.

From his rock beside Eade, Clay Forrest considered the girl and stroked his moustache with an unconscious action of gnarled fingers.

'That young man down there,' said the girl. 'He's been a Rebel soldier, hasn't he?'

Travis Eade stared hard and Forrest ceased stroking his moustache.

'What makes you ask that?' hedged Eade.

'The things he said when he rambled. He kept talking, on and on and on. He raved about fighting in battles and mentioned Manassas. That's a Confederate name. Federals call the two battles at Manassas First Bull Run and Second Bull Run.'

Clay Forrest asked: 'What if he was a Southern soldier?' There was a hard belligerence in the question, which caused the girl to fix Forrest with a steady, questioning gaze. She was mighty shrewd, thought Eade, mighty clever at putting two and two together from the ramblings of a delirious man. Young Clyman had been a mere boy when the first major battle of the war was fought at the place the Yankees called Bull Run, Virginia, in the spring of '61. He hadn't been there, but his elder brother was and he was killed in the earliest brush with the smart-alecky Yankees in their fanciful uniforms with elegant French kepis and Turkish turbans. The battle turned into a rout with the tough Johnny Rebels pushing General Irvin McDowell's raw, comic-opera soldiers back to Washington in a panicky mob. Young Dan Clyman took the death of his brother badly, especially when everyone spoke of the battle in which it had occurred as a mighty victory for the South. Dan packed his gear in the summer of '61 and sneaked away from the family's hard-scratch Texas farmstead, taking his meagre years to the nearest Confederate enlisting station.

Now, as he lay in delirium, he had talked about the place where his brother had died and he had called it by the name the Southerners used, thus alerting the girl.

'Well?' pressed Forrest. 'What if he has been a Confederate soldier. What does that matter?'

'It doesn't matter much to me,' answered the girl quietly. 'Except that it would be a pity if he should die out here under these circumstances now that the war is over and done with.'

The quietly spoken words seemed to slam across the distance between the girl and the Confederate officers with the power of skilfully thrown prize-fighter's blows. For an instant, both men were stunned by them. '. . . now that the war is over and done with . . .' the girl had said.

Travis Eade framed his questions with what he hoped was an air of carelessness: 'What do you mean by that? Do you mean the fighting has stopped?'

'Yes, the fighting has stopped,' she answered. 'Surely you heard that General Lee surrendered to General Grant early this month!' There was nothing particularly boastful or gloating in the manner in which the girl spoke the words. It was simply the fact that she spoke them with a Yankee intonation and there was something close to blasphemy in the thought that Robert E. Lee, of all men, would

surrender to the enemy which made Clay Forrest
come to his feet abruptly.

'It isn't true!' he snorted. 'It can't be true!' He
glared at the slender girl with a scowl of fury
stamped on his heavy face.

Travis Eade remained seated on his rock.
Thoughts were swirling in a crazed confusion inside
his brain. He tried to picture Lee knuckling down to
Grant. It didn't seem credible. Grant was tough and
a determined, thrusting species of general. But Lee
was cleverer. Lee was made of brains, skill and
courage. Lee would never surrender.

Eade asked: 'Where did it happen, this surrender?'

'A place in Virginia, called Appomattox Court
House. Just a little village, I believe,' replied the girl.
'Surely you've heard about it. Everyone knows about
it.'

'We've been on the desert for a long time, Ma'am,'
Eade reminded her. 'There are no newspapers in the
places we've been grubbing around in the last few
weeks.'

'I don't believe it,' declared Forrest again. 'I don't
believe Lincoln has won the war!' He spoke with the
doggedness of a wilful child. 'I just ain't goin' to
believe it!'

'President Lincoln is dead,' said the girl. 'He was
shot dead.'

Eade, still seated, and Forrest, standing in a
spraddle-legged, stubborn pose, stared at her
bleakly.

'How come,' asked Eade dully, 'that Lincoln has
been shot dead if the war and the fighting is over
and done with?'

She turned her back, moved away to the cluster of rocks where she had first sat as a lonely figure when her party entered this rock protected sink and found her travelling bag. She opened it, produced a folded newspaper and brought it back to Eade and Forrest. She thrust it into Eade's hands.

It was a copy of the *New York Herald* for 15 April 1865. Each column of its front pace was ruled off with a heavy mourning band and the leading column read:

'IMPORTANT.
ASSASSINATION OF PRESIDENT LINCOLN.
The President shot at the theatre last evening.'

Eade and Forrest read it with incredulity. Subsidiary headings were piled one upon the other for almost half of the leading column: 'ESCAPE OF THE ASSASSINS – Intense excitement in Washington. Scene at the deathbed of Mr Lincoln. – J. Wilkes Booth, the actor, the alleged assassin of the President.'

Eade and Forrest read the closely printed lines avidly, the words conjuring up a vivid picture of turbulent events in Washington. They were so engrossed in the newspaper that they did not notice the remainder of their party, Mapes, Forman, Tucker and Wain, gathering around them, attracted by their grave faces. The Confederates crowded about the newspaper, craning their necks to read it.

Sergeant Haggerty, with the remainder of his escort company and the civilian coach driver and guard, had set about hauling the dead, Apache and white, off to one side of the rock cluster, but the shrewd California Column non-com. had not failed to notice the pre-occupation of the company of 'prospectors' gathered around Eade.

Travis Eade suddenly became aware of the men standing about him with dulled faces.

'This young lady says the war is all over,' he rumbled mechanically. 'She says Lee has surrendered to Grant and this paper seems to point to the truth of it.'

'It ain't true,' murmured Clay Forrest. 'It *can't* be true!'

Corporal George Wain canted his long, angular body forward and stabbed a finger at a column in the paper.

'Don't say nothin' about any surrender,' Wain drawled with a truculent rasp to his voice. 'Says there: "Jeff Davis at Danville. – He Vainly Promises to Hold Virginia at All Hazards. – Lee and His Army Supposed to be Safe".' Wain read the words slowly, with the difficulty of a Southern farm boy of little schooling, then he demanded in a broken voice which seemed to be that of a man close to tears: 'Where do it say anythin' about surrender? Where do it say Lee surrendered?'

'Says that Richmond has fallen,' pointed out Sergeant Abner Mapes soberly. 'Says that the Confederates suffered a severe setback at Petersburg, too. Says that Governor Vance of North Carolina is advisin' Lee to surrender on Lincoln's terms.'

'And the paper's weeks old,' put in Travis Eade. 'A lot of things could have happened since this was printed.'

'It's a damn', stinkin', lyin' Yankee paper!' blurted Corporal Charlie Tucker, oblivious to the presence of the girl and to the fact that Haggerty and his blue-coats were now clustered close by, watching them with interest. 'I ain't goin' to believe no lyin' Yank paper.'

'Nor me!' put in Forrest, still holding to his mule-like stubbornness. 'I'm a Missouri man an' Missouri men don't believe nothin' till they *see* proof. That blasted New York paper ain't proof enough for me. Bobby Lee would never surrender!'

'I'm not so sure.' Eade answered wearily. 'I'm not sure at all.' He dropped the paper to the dust and began to recall a certain July day nearly two years before. . . .

FOUR

Major Travis Eade remembered how they'd been there for almost three days, in those sun-washed farmlands close to the Pennsylvania town named Gettysburg. The July sun was high, but there was a threat of rain in the air. Funny, he reflected as he and his troop fell back for a brief respite, that you could smell the wind at all in the midst of the billowing cannon smoke that the battling lines of blue and grey had brought to this place.

He remembered the unnerving rattle of those English manufactured missiles, the Whitworth bolts, screaming through the air; he remembered the pounding of Confederate Napoleon cannon and the answering thunder of Yankee artillery up there among the graves on the high line of Cemetery Ridge: he remembered the harsh shriek of the Rebel yell from the waves of ragged Southerners; he remembered the cries of dying men.

He remembered his commander, General Dick Ewell, who had taken over Stonewall Jackson's troops after Jackson had been mortally wounded by his own picquets in the fury of Chancellorsville earlier that year. Ewell, reputed to be the hardest swearer in the Confederate Army, for all he had lately got religion, came upon Eade and his men as they caught their breath in a knot of trees. The general was riding his horse, managing to grip his saddle with the stump of the leg that the Yankees had shot off in one of the first clashes of the war and with his crutches tied across his back. Eade remembered how Dick Ewell took off his hat and dashed perspiration from his famous bald head. He remembered how there was no swearing from Dick Ewell when he spoke to the young cavalry officer from Texas. Rather, there was a hushed and near reverent quality in the old warrior's voice.

'Now, Major, this is a place you'll remember all your life, if you're spared,' the general had said. 'And I declare you're about to see a sight you'll never forget.'

He waved his hat over to his left, indicating a long line of trees. Through the fog of drifting smoke, Eade saw soldiers in the trees – a mass of Southerners gathering to form a broad front, rank upon rank of them. The sun flashed on the steel of bayonets. There were ragged grey uniforms and butternut homespun, there were tattered remnants of Yankee uniforms picked up from various battlefields, there were oddments of civilian attire, there were old warriors with beards and there were young boys without shoes, there were bayonets, bayonets, bayonets, needling the sunny greenery of the trees in hundreds.

'General Pickett is rallying his men to take Cemetery Ridge,' said Dick Ewell.

Eade and his cavalrymen watched the drama of it unfold before their eyes. They saw General Pickett come out of the trees on horseback, his head held high so that his beard waved in the wind. They saw the signal of his quickly upthrust sword as he sent his mount bounding forward. They heard a single voice, a youthful one shouting on a high, near hysterical note: *'We'll follow you, Marse George! We'll follow you!'*

Then they were following him, coming out of the trees in a steadily moving mass with the battle banner of the South waving high at intervals. The grey wave moved forward into the smoke-dimmed meadowland under the rise of Cemetery Ridge. Along the Yankee-held ridge, artillery was growling, but the ranks of men continued their progress leaving here and there a stricken man squirming on the ground or a dead one lying still in its wake.

Abruptly, the harsh scream of the Rebel yell ripped along the whole length of the advancing line and Pickett's men were running up Cemetery Ridge in a surging wave of steel-tipped fury. Their objective was a low white wall, backed by a stand of trees. There were hundreds of Yankees up there on the ridge and cannon and muskets were blasting a maddening racket from the Union position. Eade and his cavalry troop watched Pickett's charge break under the onslaught of fire. They saw grey bodies littering the rise of Cemetery Ridge like the thrownback flecks of foam of a wave dashed against an indestructible rock. But there were still 'stars and bars' flying amid the smoky chaos on the ridge, still Confederate bayonets glistening in the sun; still voices screeching the Rebel yell in a crazy defiance and still clots of grey forcing themselves through the blossoming Yankee fire towards the wall.

And Pickett's charge died completely as the last lonesome foamflecks of butternut and grey and the last bobbing red banner of the South with its blue St. Andrew's cross and white stars were swallowed by the ocean of blue troops beyond the cemetery wall.

The sight haunted Travis Eade. That night, when the three days at Gettysburg were chalked up as a Yankee victory and Lee made his escape southwards, when the threatened rain had become a reality and the remains of Lee's Army of Northern Virginia slogged its weary way through mud and rain with a wagon train forty-two miles long and laden with wounded, cursing and whimpering men, Eade rode with the cavalry who covered the retreat. He remembered what men said about Pickett's charge during that miserable trek out of Pennsylvania. They claimed Pickett took no less than fifteen thousand men up the ridge.

And Eade realized something the truth of which he would be a long time in admitting. He had seen more than a military movement which had failed that day: he had seen the last of the Confederacy's youthful, energetic manhood go to its doom. Subsequent developments proved him right. After Gettysburg, the South was recruiting old men and young boys – all of them undernourished – to its ranks. Only a fool would maintain that the Confederacy could win this war when he considered what the South was fighting with after the twin defeats at Gettysburg and Vicksburg. Major Travis Eade was a fool with the rest of them and held that the seceded states would be the victors.

But, ever since that July day in '63, when he saw

Pickett's men slaughtered on Cemetery Ridge, the hidden question gnawed at the back of his mind: how long could it last?

As he sat on the rock in the dried-out water sink on the Arizona desert, the question came back to him. Perhaps it had been the same with old Bobby Lee. Perhaps that grey-bearded old Virginian who sat his horse with his lips moving in prayer as the men of the South filed past him towards the thunders and smoke of battle had seen enough courageous, doomed attacks such as Pickett's; enough brash youngsters without even shoes managing Springfield muskets almost as big as themselves and enough palsied old men who could scarcely shoulder a musket. Perhaps there was a time when a halt must be called to the folly and slaughter. Was it all that dishonourable to want to cease throwing lives away?

A fighting strain ran through Travis Eade's structure like rich sap in a pine tree. His kin had been among the first in Austin's Colony in Texas. They'd carried the banner of rebellion against the power of Mexico, they'd died at The Alamo and Coliad and cracked Mexican skulls at San Jacinto. Eade was a fighting man cut from the old rock of Texas, but he was wise enough to know when the fighting should stop. But, if the girl was speaking the truth and Lee had surrendered, what was to happen to the gold which he and his party were transporting to the Confederate coffers? The newspaper had stated plainly enough that Richmond had fallen and the President of the Confederate States had retreated to Danville with his cabinet. Was there still some form of Southern government at Danville – or had the whole structure of the Confederacy withered since that Yankee paper was printed?

Travis Eade came back to the reality of the situation. When this matter was considered on a first-things-first basis, there was no telling if any of them were going to get out of this parched rock cluster alive. Quino and his warriors had hit a lick for the far rocks and holed up there. But no one was fool enough to imagine that he'd seen the last of the Apaches. There would be desert warriors posted on those distant high rims, watching the old *tinaja* closely. Quino wanted to make a killing and he would do it either swiftly or at his ease. He might keep the whites penned up for days, but he certainly had no intention of letting them jump out of his clutches.

The day dragged on.

The situation began to fester. Almost without realising it, the whites had split themselves into factions. There was Eade and the remainder of his party; there were the California Column troopers with their sergeant and corporal and the two civilians who'd managed the coach: there was the girl, no-one seemed to know her name – the soldiers and the coach wranglers probably did, but they had cut themselves off at one corner of the waterhole while the girl spent a good deal of time down on the sink bottom attending to Clyman. She did not seem to belong to the bluecoats' faction, and she did not belong to the tattered party of supposed prospectors. She was wholly independent with a certain elegant poise which spoke of her rightful place being far from this arid land of dust, rocks and catclaw.

Eade's men sat in a knot, sullenly watching the empty spaces beyond the protecting rock wall. They did a good deal of muttering among themselves, just as Sergeant Haggerty, Corporal Hertz and the troopers muttered in their section of the rocks. Eade was conscious of occasional glances shot towards his party from the knot of bluecoats and the two civilians. Enquiring, suspicious – and often hostile – glances.

In his own group, Eade was encountering a grinding friction of personalities. Captain Clay Forrest spearheaded the trouble.

He inclined his head towards the bed of the sink where the girl had gone down to the wagon containing Clyman – and the hidden bullion.

'If what she says is right – an' I ain't prepared to believe it on the proof of a damyank paper – but if it just happened to be right, what happens to us?' he asked Eade in surly tones. 'An' what happens to that gold?'

'I don't know,' confessed Eade. 'I just don't know. I can't see the Yankees printing lies about Lincoln being shot and the fall of Richmond just for fun and, if Petersburg and Richmond have fallen to the Yankees as that paper says, then I'd say the Confederacy is finished.'

'That's damned defeatist talk,' rumbled Abner Mapes. 'Maybe with Lincoln dead there's somebody else in power in Washington who's willing to allow the Confederacy to exist as a separate nation.' That was a wild hope and Mapes seemed to know it even as he spoke the words.

Eade shook his head. 'No, Lincoln might have been the biggest Yankee of all, but Yankees are still

Yankees and they'll still hold out for Union principles.'

'That means there'll be no quarter for us,' said Charlie Tucker, his face pulled into a lugubrious expression of despair. 'I ain't goin' to live under no Yankee rule. No, sir, I'll fight 'em alone first!'

'Got to get out of this hole first,' observed Ben Forman soberly. 'But there ain't no tellin' what we'll walk into if we do get out. The Yankees might hang every man who fought for the South. After all, they claim all secesh troops are guilty of treason!'

'Too many of us to hang,' George Wain said. 'There must be someone still fightin' somewhere. General Bedford Forrest, I'll bet he's still fightin' Yankees somewhere. I'll bet General Wade Hampton is, too. He wouldn't knuckle down to the Yankees. If we bust loose out of here, I say we should find some secesh general that's still fightin' an' join him!' Wain spoke with an almost childish burst of enthusiasm, then he fell silent as though he realized he was building up an empty fantasy.

'That gold,' said Clay Forrest. 'What do we do with the gold?'

Travis Eade gave a long sigh. 'Tell you what I aim to do,' he began slowly. 'I aim to get out of here alive and put plenty of distance between me and Quino's Apaches – then I'll try to figure out the right thing to do with the bullion if it's true that the South has collapsed.'

'That don't answer the question,' rapped Forrest. There was a hard, challenging light in his eyes. 'That don't answer the question at all. You wouldn't figure the right thing to do would be to hand it over to the Yankee authorities, would you?'

'Can't say,' Eade responded. 'I honestly can't say.
As I just told you, I'm not going to consider the
matter until I'm clear of this place and all of us are
safe – if we're ever lucky enough to be in that position!'

Forrest saw the cold logic of Eade's attitude and
considered it for a minute, rubbing his moustache
thoughtfully.

'I don't like the way that girl keeps hangin'
around the wagon,' he said. 'She's tendin' to Clyman
an' that's all right, but she might just discover those
bullion cases cached on the bed of the wagon – an'
she's a Yankee for sure!'

'I'll go down and see how Clyman is making out,'
Eade told them.

He rose and walked off to the slope giving on to
the bottom of the water sink.

He passed the knot of Yankees as he did so. They
did not speak.

But the sergeant, the corporal, the troopers and
the pair of civilians watched him closely and suspi-
ciously as he went.

FIVE

The girl was standing by the wagon down on the shale of the drought-cracked bottom of the dried-up sink. The place scorched under the high sun; the closely tethered horses near the wagon had fouled the floor of the *tinaja* and flies buzzed annoyingly. In the midst of the noisome crudity of this overpopulated scratch on a wilderness map, the girl was a note of cool freshness.

It wasn't that she had to act a part to bring that note to this clump of rocks and cactus wherein they sweated until Quino's savages launched their next attack. She just had a quality of natural calm and reserve that made her a woman in a million with whom to be trapped in such a situation. She had courage, too, reflected Eade, remembering the way she had waded into the Indian fight with a blazing Derringer. She was a woman in a million, whoever she was.

She smiled at Eade as he drew close to the wagon. The sun had caught the tip of her nose and a flake of skin was beginning to peel off it. Her large dark eyes had a brightness which matched the high

57

sheen of her black hair, escaping from the confines of the poke bonnet.

Eade looked under the canvas awning which protected Dan Clyman from the sun. He saw that the injured man was still sleeping and that the girl had taken clothing from her travelling bag to fashion a soft pillow under his head.

'I think he'll be much better when he awakens,' the girl said softly. 'He slept right through the fight when the Indians got in here. I'm only glad they didn't harm him.'

'And I'm glad you're around to look after him the way you are,' Eade answered. 'Many another woman in a fix like this would sit down and weep and be a general hindrance. My men and I are mighty grateful for the help you've given young Clyman.'

'Weeping would not help at all,' said the girl gravely. 'Even if we never get out of here alive, weeping wouldn't make it one bit better.'

Eade's sharp eyes caught a glimpse of dark wings high against the blaze of the sun. He looked up casually and tried not to betray his feelings as he watched the buzzard circle in a lonesome manoeuvre away above their heads. The scavenger bird had been attracted there by the bodies of the whites and Apaches killed in the fight. He wondered how soon there would be more of them – not winging expectantly above them, but squatting among these rocks, tearing the flesh off the corpses of all of them.

The girl did not see the high floating buzzard. She asked: 'Is that his name – Clyman?'

'Dan Clyman,' Eade informed her. He deemed it better not to add that the injured youngster was a corporal in the Confederate Army. Instead, he introduced himself: 'And I'm Travis Eade, the fellow who's in charge of the prospecting outfit.'

She looked at him with something like a mocking wisdom in her eyes.

'Are you really a band of prospectors?' she asked. Eade felt his heart take two beats in the space of one. He wondered if she had come across the heavy bullion cases hidden at the bottom of the wagon during her tending of Clayman. She did not wait for any answer but went on to introduce herself.

'My name is Marguerite Norman. I'm on my way home to New York. I was governess to the children of an aristocratic family in Mexico until the war became so bad that the family decided I had best return home.'

'The war?' asked Eade, not following the girl.

'Not the war between the states,' she told him. 'I mean the other war – the one that's going on in Mexico.'

Eade remembered that the French, in a moment of supreme impudence, had sent an invading force to Mexico and attempted to set up a French puppet emperor. A second war, one between French and Mexicans, raged south of the Rio Grande while the war between the states was reaching its final stages. Eade and his party had been so long cut off from any source of news that this Mexican war had slipped their memories.

'I reached Nogales, where there is a stage terminus for Fort McDowell and Prescott. There were some other Americans there but when the soldiers escorting the coach said there'd been a massacre when the Apaches caught up with an earlier coach leaving Prescott, they decided not to travel. I was the only one who'd risk it.' She looked up suddenly, saw the buzzard for the first time and added: 'Now I wish I had stayed in Nogales with the others.'

To Travis Eade's discomfort, Marguerite Norman changed the subject abruptly: 'Is it true what the cavalry sergeant is saying about you?'

'What's he saying?'

'I don't want to create any trouble between you, but I heard him say to the corporal that you'd all bear watching. He said that you personally were shouting Rebel yells during the fight with the Apaches and that the whole bunch of you talked like Southerners, so he figured you were a party of Rebel deserters headed for Mexico. He thinks you might be Confederates out of Texas who've sneaked away because the South was being beaten.'

Eade felt his ire rising. A dim recollection that he bellowed the Confederacy's battle cry during the fight with the Apaches seeped back to him and he cursed himself for it. That shrewd, bearded sergeant, Haggerty, was suspicious. Next thing they knew, he'd be nosing about the wagon and discovering the gold!

'I don't care what you are,' the girl added quickly. 'You all fought tremendously during the Indian attack. I don't think you look like men who'd run away just because things were going badly with your cause. Even if you are ex-Confederates, I don't see that it should make any difference to any of us, holed up here in a little world of our own.'

'That makes sense,' murmured Eade. 'This is not the time and place to fight out the war.'

'The war's over. It's already been fought out,' Marguerite Norman reminded him. 'We should remember what Mr Lincoln said just before he died.'

'What did he say?'

'That newspaper I showed you was just one of a bundle my sister sent from New York. There were others I left in Mexico. One of them had a story that told how Mr Lincoln came out of the White House just after the news of Lee's surrender broke out. The people cheered him and there was a band standing by, all ready to play a tune. Mr Lincoln called out: 'We are one people now. Bid the band play "Dixie",' and that's what they played.'

'He said that, did he?' rumbled Eade thoughtfully. 'Old Abe said that and a Yankee band played "Dixie" outside the White House?' The thought gave him a glimpse of Lincoln in a new light, one in which he had never seen the long, lean and melancholy Yankee President before.

'We are one people,' repeated Marguerite Norman gravely. 'One people cooped up in this pile of rocks. As you said, this is not the time or place to fight the war.'

She glanced upwards and saw the wheeling buzzard again.

For the first time, her face showed something resembling fear.

'Do you think we'll get out of here alive?' she asked Eade.

The Texan shrugged his shoulders. 'We stand a chance, but we won't get clear without a hard fight. The best thing to do is not to think ahead. Take whatever comes as it comes and keep your mind off what might be coming up in the immediate future.'

It was with a wisdom learned in battle that he spoke, but the dark haired girl had already absorbed some of that same wisdom by her brief experience here.

'I know,' she nodded. 'That's why helping this injured man is so important to me – it keeps my mind off how scared I am. If I didn't have something to do, I'd die of sheer fright.'

'I doubt it,' commented Travis Eade. He was of the opinion that the slight girl, in her now soiled, once elegant dress, had a courage that would stand even if Cochise himself and all his Chiricahua Apaches swooped down on the old water-hole.

He left her standing by the wagon and climbed the sides of parched *tinaja*. The two sets of defenders, each apart from the other, sat in the sun-pounded rocks, heads low, carbines gripped across their knees and their eyes scrunched in the direction of the rearing rims in which Quino's warriors were hidden. In the prospectors' group, Clay Forrest appeared to be holding sway, talking in a voice that was little more than a whisper while Mapes, Forman, Tucker and Wain listened. Forrest was being watched with an undiguised interest by both Sergeant Haggerty and Corporal Hertz who, with their bluecoated companions and the civilian coachmen, were too far away to hear what the Captain was saying.

Forrest ceased his talking when he saw Eade approaching and gave his attention to the distant rims with exaggerated intensity. Eade squatted on a rock close to him.

'Clyman's sleeping,' he said mechanically. 'He might be in better shape when he wakens.'

Forrest gave a grunt which might have meant anything and continued staring at the rearing rims across the shimmering floor of the desert. Sergeant Haggerty rose and walked across from his sector of the rocks protecting the dried-out sink. His weathered face was set in stern lines and his earlier hail-fellow-well-met air seemed to have slipped from him like a discarded cloak. He squatted close to Eade's party, hunkering behind the protective rocks so that the brass sabres crossed on his forage cap did not show in a sun-touched glare, marking his position for the watching Apaches in the rims.

'See here, you fellows. I have a theory about you an' there ain't much use in concealin' it,' said the sergeant. 'I figure you ain't prospectors at all, but Johnny Rebels headed for Mexico now that the war is finished. You all talk like Southerners and you, Mr Eade, were hollerin' Rebel yells when the Apaches got in here. I ain't complainin' about you bein' Rebs. though—'

'Then what're you squattin' there talkin' about it for?' cut in Clay Forrest sharply. The Confederate captain's heavy face was pulled into an ominous scowl. Eade felt that the slowly grinding friction that had started building up between these assorted men might flare into more tangible trouble at this point, but it was held down by the cavalry sergeant who continued slowly: 'I ain't complainin' about what you might be. We're all in this box together an' we're all white men.' He paused, threw a glance over his shoulder to the parched sink on the bottom of which stood Marguerite Norman.

'There's another matter, one we might as well be clear on. As the non com. in charge of the coach escort, I'm responsible for that young woman's safety. There were other whites at Nogales who were to make the trip to Prescott but they all cried off. Only that girl had the courage – or foolhardiness – to risk it. I just want to put it to you fellows that she don't fall into the hands of Quino's devils if they should swamp us an' if I should get killed. It's somethin' I'll take care of myself if I'm able, but if I ain't, I'll rely on one of my men or one of you to see they don't get her alive.'

There was a cold and terrible logic in the suggestion. Eade knew that it made sense in the way that many things which upset the nicely balanced outlook of the cities made sense out here on the frontier.

He knew how the Apaches would treat a captive white woman and death from a cleanly aimed bullet was far preferable, but he felt a cold twist at his stomach at the thought conjured up by the soldier's words. He was aware that he would not have the courage to take it upon himself to kill Marguerite Norman and he felt, rather than saw, a ripple of shocked dismay flow through his own small party.

'She did pretty well in the fight with that little pistol,' drawled Abner Mapes. 'That young woman is mighty valuable.'

'I agree,' Haggerty said. 'She's worth a dozen of plenty women I've met. I don't like to think about it any more than you do – but don't let any of us get elevated knowin' we're the last to die an' she's still alive. Quino will kill us clean an' spread little bits of us out in the sun for the buzzards – but he'll have different ideas about the girl.'

The sergeant moved back to his men, leaving Eade, Forrest, Mapes, Forman, Wain and Tucker squatting together in a leaden silence. Out across the flat desert, distorted by the dancing heat-hazes, the rims which sheltered Quino's watching Apaches rose harsh and timeless against the burnished azure of the sky. Nothing stirred within the scatter of rocks which guarded the old water-hole. There was not even a familiar rock lizard to come out of hiding and stare at the men who had invaded the place.

The defenders hunkered close to the rocks, trying to make use of scant shade which would scarcely give comfort to a jackrabbit. They felt the sting of the sun bite through their clothing and it heated buckles and weapon barrels as though they had been held long before a glowing fire.

There was no sound save the occasional snort and pawing of a fractious and nervous horse tethered down on the dusty floor of the old sink.

There were now two buzzards up in the sky.

SIX

They came to the edge of evening and there was no attack from the Apaches. Eade and his party were huddled close together in the rocks, eyes straining across the expanse of wasteland which stretched between them and the rims. The desert was silent and the air held an electric, climbing tension.

'Maybe they ain't goin' to attack,' ventured Charlie Tucker. 'Maybe they've had all the sport they want an' have just left us. Maybe we could ride out of here in peace and quiet.'

'Not a hope,' Eade told him. 'When 'Paches jump whites and hole them up the way we've been holed up, they wait their chance to finish 'em off. They're watching us from those rimrocks yonder and if we attempted to run from here we'd have a couple of dozen of the varmints on our tails.'

'We might be able to spring out of this place after dark,' suggested Clay Forrest.

'That's a vain hope, too,' Eade answered. 'They'll be more alert after dark than they are now, expecting us to attempt something like sneaking away under cover of the night. There'll be Indians prowling around these rocks after sundown for sure.'

A gloomy silence fell upon them and Travis Eade began to reflect upon the knowledge brought by this encounter with their desert-travelling fellow whites. So the war was over and the Confederate States were whipped. It came as no surprise, now that he could reflect upon it; the defeat was simply the fulfilment of the prophecy Travis had seen at Gettysburg when Pickett's men went up Cemetery Hill in their screaming waves.

The news helped to clarify the situation in regard to the gold, also. That incoherent message of Gribbon's, scrawled on the wall of the abandoned mission, might be a gesture of despair. Somewhere along the way to the rendezvous with the bullion, Gribbon and his party had heard about the defeat of the South. With Mexico torn by its fight against the French invaders, there might have been too much risk in taking the gold back south of the border. Burying it in the mission could have been a final desperate act before the party disappeared somewhere in Mexico rather than venture into the country in which the hated bluecoats of Lincoln had been victorious.

The gold was on Clay Forrest's mind, too. He edged nearer to Eade and whispered in a confidential tone: 'Maybe we could get clear of this place with the wagon, just the seven of us, an' make it to Mexico. You heard what the Yankee sergeant said about plenty of Rebs runnin' for Mexico now that the war's over. Maybe we could risk it after sundown.'

Eade knew a cold stirring of distaste at the way in which Forrest suggested it. It would be impossible to leave this *tinaja* without the vigilant, bloodthirsty warriors knowing it. Even if it were possible, he could not run out and leave the remainder of the party. He told Forrest so.

'Them?' asked Forrest with a note of scorn in his voice. 'Them Yankees? You ain't considerin' them! Our business is to look out for ourselves an' to hell with them Yankees.'

Unbidden, the memory of what the young woman, Marguerite Norman, had said about their being one people rose in Eade's mind. He recalled that Sergeant Haggerty had hauled a savage away from him when the Apache was about to strangle him. He could never desert the remainder of the whites with whom they were stranded and the mistrust he had always felt of Captain Clay Forrest deepened at that moment. Forrest had courage, he would have risked the storm of Apache arrows in a crazy attempt to get to Dufay when that first victim of their battle with the Indians fell from his mount; equally he had a stubborn and brutal streak. Eade realized during this short conversation that Forrest had it in him to desert the remainder of the party merely because they were Yankees.

'That's a stupid suggestion,' Eade told him. 'There's no getting out of here without Quino's Apaches seeing us – and we won't desert these other people.'

'You speak for yourself,' Forrest rasped, ill temper flaring in his eyes. 'I have no love for Yankees. There's no tellin' how the damyanks will treat us now the war's over an' we're defeated. That blue-belly sergeant thinks we're doomed, you heard what he said about the woman. Well, he can be massacred, but I don't intend to be. I aim to stay alive without worryin' too much about the safety of any Yankees!'

'I don't see it that way,' Eade growled. 'Anyway, one of them is a woman. We can't leave them.'

'What the hell difference does a woman make?' Forrest wanted to know. He was sprawled against the shale and rock, instinctively keeping his head below the protecting wall of rock. His dark eyes had gone almost black with anger and his harshly whispered words were causing curiosity among the Yankee cavalrymen squatting amid their cluster of rocks some yards away. They could not hear what passed between the two, but they were aware that an argument had flared. 'I got no call to bother my head about Yankee women,' Forrest went on. 'I'm from Missouri, remember, I was fightin' damned abolitionists even before this war started. When those Kansas jayhawkers came over the border into Missouri, they killed an' injured some of my kin. One of 'em was my brother's wife – she was killed. Why should I worry about what happens to any Yankee woman?'

Travis Eade made no reply. There was no point in fighting this thing out with Forrest. His attitude was coloured by the brutal background against which he had lived almost all his life. He came out of the roiling border wars between Missouri and Kansas which had raged over the issue of slavery since the presidency of Franklin Pierce and which had been going on for almost a decade when the whole nation split into civil war.

Forrest had belonged to the 'Border Ruffians', the band of brutal raiders from pro-slavery Missouri who foraged into 'bleeding Kansas' to war against

the anti-slavery 'free soil' men of that region. He had
been with the bloodthirsty bunch which marched on
the no-slavery stronghold of Lawrence, Kansas,
trailing a cannon with which to terrorize the place
on a certain day in 1855. Such action brought retal-
iation from the border raiders of Kansas, the rabid
no-slavery men called 'jayhawkers' who did not stop
at murder, looting and burning when they raided
into Missouri.

This tumultuous life in the boiling pot of the
middle border had made a Yankee-hating ruffian of
Clay Forrest as much as the wide-open challenge of
Texas life had made Travis Eade into a devil-be-
damned warrior with a broad streak of indepen-
dence and wide horizons of the mind.

Clay Forrest glowered at Eade, the red glow of the
now declining sun putting a crimson edge to one
side of his face and the pugnacious bristle of his
moustache.

'You're on their blamed side,' complained Forrest.
'On the side of those damned Yankees!'

'It isn't a matter of sides. In a hole like this, we're
one people,' Eade answered. He reiterated the words
the girl said Abraham Lincoln had used almost
unconsciously. There was a simple grandeur in them
which seemed out of place here, as well as a simple
logic which seemed wasted on one with Clay
Forrest's bull-headed stubbornness. 'There's no such
thing as Yankee and Reb between us in a fix like
this,' contended Eade. 'Anyway, we couldn't possibly
hitch up our wagon and haze out of here. The whole
notion is plumb impossible.'

'On their damned side,' repeated Forrest as
though he had not even heard what Eade had said.

'Wouldn't surprise me if you didn't see fit to declare that we're carryin' bullion an' hand it over to those Yankees. Talk about us all bein' one is just hogwash. A damyank is a damyank an' always will be to me!' He spat into the dry shale as if to add a heavy emphasis to the opinion.

The remainder of the Confederate band sat or sprawled on the rocks close by, half watching the desert, now painted garish reds and purples under the reddening, lowering sun and half interested in the low whispering and growling of the two officers at odds. Mapes, Tucker, Wain and Forman took in the argument, keeping their own counsel. Each was, in his own way, aware that there was a breaking down of relationships in this situation. They had started out as officers and non-commissioned officers of the Confederate Army. But now, if the news the California Column troopers and the girl had given them was true, that army existed no longer. Each of them wondered how soon the situation among them would deteriorate down to one in which ranks were forgotten and it became simply a matter of every man for himself.

The dying sun filled the sky with a hundred hues of red, purple and gold-lined azure. A wind with a knife edge of chilliness came off the desert and stalked the tumbled rocks of the old water hole.

Night descended, cold by contrast with the blaze of day and menacing in this silence.

Marguerite Norman had rummaged in her travelling bag and produced a heavy shawl of wool which she had wrapped about her against the biting chill of the night. She made a dark, huddled hump in the

rocks as she slithered to a squatting position beside
Travis Eade who sat with his party, cradling his
carbine across his knees and staring into the blackness of the desert.

'Clyman is awake,' she told Eade. 'He's got over
the delirium, but he's confused about this situation.
He asked for you.' She paused, as though inwardly
debating whether she should say more, then quickly
added: 'He called you "Major Eade".'

Eade answered: 'Did he?' as if it were a matter of
no consequence. He rose on legs that had become
stiffened by the seeping cold of the desert night. He
was aware that Forrest, Wain, Forman, Mapes and
Tucker, sitting as silent as the rocks which
surrounded them, were watching him – watching, at
least, the tall silhouette he made as he stood
upright.

'I'll come down to the wagon,' he told the girl
quietly.

'Damn Yankee woman,' snorted Forrest to no one
in particular. 'She's cottoned on to him bein' a major
an' that sergeant has figured we're Rebels. Next
thing we know, them Yankees an' the Apaches will
be joinin' forces to capture us an' share whatever
reward the Washington government is givin' for
good, hang-able Confederates.'

Ben Forman shuffled his feet in the darkness.

'You figure that's what the Washington government will do – hang all Johnny Rebs?' he asked.
Then he answered his own question hurriedly: 'Hell,
they couldn't do that. There's too many of us!'

'We lost the war, an' we were in rebellion accordin'
to their book,' opined Forrest. 'I wouldn't put nothin'
past Yankees – nothin'! They might hang us all, or

shoot us all or they might put shackles on us an' make us work in the fields while the blacks they freed whip us.'

The cold, eerie darkness of the desert night seemed to bring a frightening reality to their fantasies of Southern life under the rule of the victorious Yankees. There was a tight silence, then George Wain drawled: 'Hell, I'd rather be killed by 'Paches than have that happen!'

'I'd sooner wriggle out of here somehow an' turn around an' get to Mexico for good an' all,' Abner Mapes said.

'So would I,' Clay Forrest replied. 'I'd sooner get to Mexico – with that bullion for companionship!'

Down at the wagon on the dark-shadowed floor of the sink, Eade found Dan Clyman sitting up inside the vehicle. It was too dark for him to see his face, but he heard the youngster's heavy, pain-fretted breathing.

'Shoulder giving you much trouble?' Eade asked.

'Trouble enough, Major, but it could be worse. I guess I slept a long time. What are we doin' in this place?'

'We're boxed up by 'Paches, holed up in a dry water sink,' Eade answered. His eyes moved to the shadowy form of the girl standing beside the wagon. With a deliberate slowness, he added: 'We're in here with a vedette of Fort McDowell cavalry. We met up with them on the desert just when the Indians showed up and tried to jump the whole bunch of us.'

He heard the youthful corporal catch his breath and told him: 'Just you lie there and take it easy. So long as you lie right where you are, I guess everything will be all right. We'll probably sweat out this

Indian attack in due time,' Eade knew that there
was a hollowness to this last opinion that showed in
his voice, but he sensed that Clyman had caught the
message he had tried to convey in the admonition to
stay where he was. The youngster was lying on top
of the bullion boxes. So long as he remained there,
he could guard the gold against any prying from the
bluecoats from Fort McDowell.

'I'll stay here,' Clyman said. 'Just give me a pistol
in case those 'Paches come callin'. I guess I could
handle a pistol easy enough.'

Travis Eade unholstered his own Navy Colt and
handed it to the youth in the wagon.

Marguerite Norman asked: 'When do you think
they'll come?' There was a sigh of weariness in her
voice which betrayed the fact that this taut, inactive
situation was beginning to tell on her. She was not a
woman who would take kindly to having ugly facts
sugar-coated, Eade thought. She had shown herself
to be tough enough to take the harsh reality of the
frontier, therefore he made no attempt to disguise
reality when he answered: 'There's no telling.
'Paches are cunning and they're cat-and-mousing
us. They might swoop any minute, on the other
hand, they might lie hidden in those rims, watching
us for days until our water runs out and we're too
weak or too crazed to fight when they attack. If I
were you, I'd hole up with a blanket from one of the
horses and get some sleep.'

Marguerite Norman gave a fastidious sniff.

*'Sleep under a blanket that's been on a horse's
back!'* she exclaimed with a high note of genuine
objection.

'What's the matter with horses?' demanded the

Texas drawl of Dan Clyman indignantly. 'I've been on tolerably good terms with plenty of horses an' there ain't nothin' objectionable about 'em!'

Travis Eade rumbled a deep laugh at the manner in which the young corporal had come to the defence of horseflesh and Marguerite Norman realized that her fastidiousness was out of place here. She matched Eade's laughter with a small, silver peal of her own.

The laughter was infectious. Dan Clyman caught its spirit and chuckled in the darkness of the interior of the wagon. There was a blessed release from tension in just laughing and they laughed for a long time.

SEVEN

There was a stirring from Clay Forrest and the remnants of the Confederate party as laughter floated up from the floor of the dried-out sink.

'A fine time for laughter,' grumbled Forrest. 'A fine time for hob-nobbin' with a Yankee woman!' He left it at that, but there was an innuendo in the observation which worked subtle mischief among the Southerners.

There was a silence then, out of the darkness, George Wain asked: 'Do you figure we could get out of here with the gold an' make it to Mexico? Maybe some of the generals have managed to get there. We might be able to join 'em. The Yankee sergeant said that Confederates had run for Mexico. Wade Hampton an' some of the others might have got there. They might want to continue the fight an' that bullion would be useful.'

'Yes, you can bet Hampton would continue fightin'. I couldn't see him buckling under to any Yankee rule,' put in Abner Mapes.

'We wouldn't want no damned Yankee-lovers along,' stipulated Forrest meaningfully.

Eade came up from the bed of the sink and was aware of the suspicious quality of their leaden silence when he joined them.

'Clyman is conscious. He's still in plenty of pain, but holding out well,' he informed them. 'Wish I could get out of this hole and take that boy to a surgeon to have that shoulder set properly.'

Someone among the huddled silhouettes grunted and that was the only reply he received.

Among the California Column troopers, squatting in their own section of rocks, there was a whispered discussion. After a time, two figures detached themselves from the rest and came over to the Southerners. They were Haggerty and Corporal Hertz. They had a proposition.

'We been talkin' over ways an' means of gettin' relieved from this fix,' the sergeant said. 'We figure a couple of men on fast horses might make a dash from here to Fort McDowell before dawn to tell the military of how we're holed-up.'

'Too risky,' objected Eade. 'You can bet there are Indians out there on the desert now. They'd hear riders taking off and go after them. Those 'Paches won't miss our slightest attempt to bust clear of this place.'

'We could muffle ringbits an' trappin's. Some of those cavalry horses tethered yonder are in good shape an' could match Apache mustangs,' Corporal Hertz said.

'Who goes?' asked the bulky silhouette of Clay Forrest.

'Our bunch has agreed to settle it on drawin' cards. The two lowest cards make the ride,' Haggerty answered.

'Seems damn risky to me,' wavered Ben Forman. 'Them 'Paches are all eyes an' ears – an' they seem to be at their best in the dark.'

Eade was reconsidering his earlier objection that the proposal was too risky.

'Their bunch has agreed to risk it on drawin' cards,' he stated with a meaningful stress. 'Are we goin' to back out of it?' Eade put the question in a way which implied that a crew of Yankees was prepared to undertake the risk while a party of Southerners dickered about it. This manner of framing the issue, brought a swift and unanimous agreement from the Confederates.

Hertz produced a deck of cards from his tunic pocket.

'Who shuffles them?' asked Eade.

'Not Hertz,' said Haggerty. 'That's an understood thing in our outfit – Hertz is never allowed to shuffle!'

Corporal Hertz grinned in the blackness.

'How about the young lady?' he suggested. 'She don't look like a cardsharp an' I guess she might put good fortune on the venture. Don't they say luck is a lady?'

'You should know – you lived with a deck of cards in your pocket all your life,' commented Haggerty drily.

The business was carried out with a quiet determination. Eade went down to the wagon, found that Marguerite Norman had overcome her objection to horse-blankets to the extent that she was now wrapped in one and lying against one of the wheels of the vehicle. He woke her with an apology and took her up the slope of the sink to a huddled group of

men. An unspoken truce existed between the two
factions now and they squatted behind a high rock,
waiting without speaking, their tensed breathing
matching the whisper of the night wind among the
rocks.

Sergeant Haggerty struck a flame with his big
flint-and-wheel cigar lighter. He cupped his hands
around it to keep it alive and the wavering flame
painted yellow highlights on the strained faces of
the men, on the gentle structure of the girl's face,
framed in the poke bonnet and on her slender
fingers as she shuffled the greasy cards. She
concluded the shuffling, squared the deck and
placed it on the shale at her feet.

The feeble flame and the men moved closer to the
ground as they squatted and craned their necks
towards the cards like hens around a succulent tit-
bit on a barnyard floor. They took a card each, reaching out solemnly one by one and turning up the
pasteboard close to the light in Haggerty's hand to
ascertain their luck.

At the first draw, four emerged with aces – which
they had agreed would count low: Eade, Hertz, one
of the civilian coachmen and a lanky, silent
California Column trooper.

'I don't like the look of four aces comin' out
together,' complained Corporal Hertz, the supersti-
tious gambling man. 'Specially when I see this kind
of ace in my own hand!' He flourished the card he
had drawn in the fitful blaze of the cigar lighter. It
was the ace of spades.

'We four draw again to decide it,' Travis Eade said
in a voice without colour. 'Shuffle again, Miss
Norman.'

She took the cards once more, shuffled them and placed them down before the four men making the deciding draw. Eade drew a seven of hearts, the lanky trooper made a relieved grimace as he turned up a card and saw a ten of clubs and the coach wrangler drew a two of spades. His weather-punished face, fringed by a greying beard, registered not the slightest emotion.

Corporal Hertz picked his card with an elegant flourish and said: '*Blazes!*' in a crackling, incredulous voice when he looked at it in the glow of the lighter.

Once more, he had drawn the jinx card, the ace of spades.

The men uncurled from their squatting positions slowly, Hertz being the last to rise. He stood silent for a moment as though stunned.

'Luck of the draw,' he said abruptly, shrugging his shoulders as it trying to shake off dozens of ace-of-spade superstitions accrued during a lifetime of gambling. 'Which horses d'you suggest we take, Sarge?'

'Take mine, he's wiry and fast,' offered the youthful trooper with the struggling moustache.

'And you take mine, Givens,' Sergeant Haggerty told the coachman. 'He's the chestnut. Both of you muffle the bits and trappin's an' walk those horses out of here on the far side of the sink. Look out for 'Paches back there as you go, some of 'em probably sneaked around there under cover of the dark so they can watch ont for just such a move as this. When you get to McDowell, tell 'em Quino is cat-an'-mousin' us. Tell 'em we have some water but darn little ammunition. Another big attack like the one they made earlier will about clean us out of bullets. Tell 'em to come runnin'. Good luck!'

Eade and his companions watched the shadowy shapes of Hertz and the taciturn Givens go down the slope of the sink to the horses. Something within him protested that it should have been two of the Southerners who took the risk of attempting to break through the net which the Apaches would now have strung around the *tinaja* in the velvet blackness. They had lost their war and they had little to live for. Why shouldn't they risk Apache arrows?

Then, an unbidden protest rose in reaction to that line of thought. They might have lost the war, but there must be something to live for. There might be hard times ahead for the South and the people of the South might want men with a strong faith in the future and the will to fight and survive.

Whatever lay ahead would be better than death at the hands of the scheming desert warriors who now held the whites under the torture of simply waiting.

From down on the bed of the sink, there came the slightest clop of moving hoofs and a horse snorted briefly.

Then, there was a long silence. The men in the rocks and cactus at the lip of the water-hole with Marguerite Norman among them, held stiff, listening poses for a long time. There was only the breath of the chill-edged desert breeze. Hertz and Givens must be clear of the rock-pile by now and they had made their exit carefully and silently. They must have fooled the alert Apaches who haunted the empty darkness beyond. . . .

Speedily, half-heard by all of them, there came a

rapid tattoo. It rode the slight breeze out of the dark distances for an instant. Then it was gone.

It sounded like Apache mustangs travelling fast, giving pursuit.

They hoped it wasn't.

EIGHT

The first fingers of dawn touched the far skies with streaks of gold and crimson which gradually spread and merged into the swelling light of day. The sun began its climb and the heat was there from the first appearance of the blazing disc as it rimmed the ragged eastern horizon.

In the rock-pile, the vigilant whites cradled their rifles and watched the appearance of day. Some of them had managed a modicum of fitful sleep, but all were awake now, crouched behind protecting rocks, wondering if this would be their last day.

The memory of those half-heard hoofbeats which had drummed out of the desert darkness so soon after Hertz and Givens had slipped away on their attempt to reach Fort McDowell remained with each of them as a disturbing, gnawing question. None of them cared to mention it to his neighbour, but each was tortured by the same query: had the Apaches caught and killed the corporal and his companion?

Travis Eade was squatting against a heat-split rock, viewing the rimrocks in the distance through slitted eyes. In those tangled rocks, separated from the *tinaja* by perhaps half a mile of heat veiled

desert, Quino and his kill-crazy braves watched and
waited their chance to play their own bloodthirsty
game with the whites. Eade could not see a sign of
feathers or breech-clouts in the rims, but he knew
there was no likelihood of the Apaches having
departed in the night.

There was, however, evidence enough that the
braves had ventured forth during the night and had
been almost within these scattered rocks without
the whites hearing their approach. After the
running fight with Eade and his men and the
onslaught against the *tinaja* the previous day,
several dead warriors had sprawled on the desert.
They had stiffened in the sun all through the day
while buzzards circled in the heat-charged blue of
the sky, not daring to land because of the presence of
living men.

Now, the newly risen sun showed that the tract
between the rock-pile and the rims was empty of
Indian dead. The Apaches had come out of their
stronghold in the darkness to cart their warriors'
bodies back for burial rites. They had been almost
into the rocks in which the whites sheltered to
remove dead warriors from the fringe of the water-
hole. They had been so near, unheard and unseen,
but they had not attacked – proof that Quino had
given orders that these holed-up whites would be
finished off the way he wanted.

Doubtless, the crazy Apache renegade was going
to take his time about it. And he would make it slow
and painful.

Travis Eade thought about their prospects of
survival as he watched dawn swelling into day. He
thought about how the water was running low. They

had checked their total supply by examining all the canteens they possessed during the night. The check revealed that careful rationing was called for.

He thought about their scanty supply of ammunition. It was true, as Sergeant Haggerty had earlier pointed out, that they had barely enough to stand off another large-scale Apache attack.

Maybe, thought Eade, the corporal and Givens had got clear away and would make it to Fort McDowell. Maybe they would be able to rouse the cavalry and bring a force which could fight off Quino's braves.

Ironically, he recalled that, up until yesterday, he had been far from pleased to see attacking blue-coated cavalry. Now, he would give a lot to set eyes on those bluecoats in their short riding jackets and their yellow seamed pants hoofing to the rescue. The pleasant prospect of such a situation developing faded when the haunting memory of those faintly drumming hoofs returned to him. They had sounded too much like unshod pony hoofs for him to fool himself about what they meant.

The Apaches were not missing the slightest move made by the besieged whites by day or night. They had been prowling the desert when Hertz and Givens left the water sink and they had given chase. This situation, thought Eade, was one in which the party of whites were as good as nailed up in their coffins and buried – except that Apaches had no use for such refinements as coffins, nor did they bury the whites they butchered. Too bad, he thought, that the girl had to be caught in this trap with them. It would have been far better if she had been a coward and stayed back at Nogales with the rest of the stage passengers when they heard of Quino's rampaging in Arizona.

Close to Eade, Captain Clay Forrest sprawled watchfully on the hot shale. Forrest's thoughts were in a turmoil. Like Eade, he acknowledged the futility of their situation. But the thought of the bullion hidden in the wagon plagued him. All that gold had to fall into someone's hands. Indians would have no use for it and it was too good for Yankee hands.

Forrest's thoughts wandered once more into the realms of fantasy. If only he and the remainder of the Confederate bunch could get clear of this sun-hammered hell hole. If only they could slither out from under those unseen Apache eyes. If only they could have that bullion to themselves without being ramrodded by Eade, a damned, wavering lady-chaser who'd spent his time last night giggling with that Yankee woman down on the sink bed!

Clay Forrest did not stop to remind himself that he and his companions, all of whom had put their heads close together in Eade's absence last night, had magnified the matter beyond all reason. As someone had said when they grumbled among themselves in the darkness, no-one would have imagined Major Travis Eade would have turned out that way, but, by thunder, that was the way he had turned out. Clay Forrest had made it clear that one officer might have dithered and thrown in his hand when he heard, on the strength of a mere Yankee newspaper and the word of a bunch of Yankees, that the South's fight was over and lost, but there was a second officer in this outfit and he was still fighting. There had been a burr of grumbling approval from the men.

Forrest knew they were with him – every man of them. To blazes with Eade and his readiness to believe what the Yankees told him and his willingness to head for Fort McDowell. His talk of getting young Clyman to a doctor was all very well, but it was only one aspect of the business. Who was to say that the Yankees at the fort would not hand over every Rebel of them to be hanged – if that was what the Washington government was doing to secesh soldiers? They might well be hanging all Rebels, thought Forrest, especially if it was true that Lincoln had been shot dead by a Confederate sympathizer. Those Yankees might go berserk and retaliate by taking the lives of all who had worn the Rebel grey. There was no knowing what the Washington men might do, especially if power had fallen to some highly-placed Yankees he could think of: Edwin Stanton, Lincoln's ugly, stringy bearded Secretary for War; plundering, burning General William T. Sherman, with his angry scowl, or cross-eyed General Benjamin Franklin Butler, who had earned the lasting hatred of every Dixielander. These and others would not give a defeated Rebel half a chance if they were in absolute power.

Even in the mounting, searing heat of the desert morning, Clay Forrest shivered at the thought.

Well, by thunder, they would not get their claws on Captain Clay Forrest. He was going to continue fighting Yankees. There must be someone still standing and shooting for the Southern cause and he was going to join whoever it was – with a load of useful bullion.

His thoughts went back to his native middle-border, to the tortured lands of Missouri and Kansas

where he had fought Yankee influences long before
General Beauregard's gunner, Edwin Ruffin, fired
the first Confederate shot at Fort Sumter and
opened the war. Three names floated into his mind,
standing out as against a blazing backcloth:
Quantrill, Todd and Anderson!

Now there were three fighters who would
continue to fight, mused Forrest. They were of the
calibre that kept up a relentless battle against the
bluecoated forces of the North, even when the rest of
the South had stopped. Spawned by the brawling,
decade-long war of the Kansas-Missouri border, the
raiders headed by Quantrill, Todd and Anderson
had attacked, plundered and burned with fearsome
abandon in the pro-Northern regions of Kansas.
They had hit their zenith in the dying days of the
summer of 1863 with the sacking and razing of the
anti-slavery stronghold of Kansas, the town of
Lawrence, that self-same town which Forrest had
raided as a youthful Missouri Border Ruffian in '55.

Forrest reflected that these three were far from
the kind given to easy surrender. If he could get to
them with the bullion, there might be a chance of
continuing his fight against the Union. Maybe they
had made it to Mexico to join others of the no-
surrender persuasion. Suppose Confederate fighters
like Wade Hampton, Longstreet, Quantrill, Todd
and Anderson and others who still had fight in them
had managed to run across the border. They'd need
money to buy supplies and ammunition and, so long
as they had supplies and slugs, they would continue
to fight!

Forrest, sprawling in the dust, straining his eyes
through the shimmering heat-waves of the desert,

built the notion into a great fantasy. The thing to do, by thunder, was to get clear of here and take that gold south of the border to whatever Confederate remnants waited there to continue their battle for the stars and bars!

He came to reality with a jarring shock.

He recalled the soft but distinct sound of unshod Indian mustangs thumping out of the velvet darkness of the desert the previous night, just after Hertz and Givens had left. Those blamed Apaches had given pursuit, all right, and there was little hope that the whites in the rock-scattered *tinaja* would ever get out of their fix alive.

Forrest fumed inwardly. It was one hell of a way to finish up! Waiting here for the butchering savages to swoop down and slaughter them was just plain foolish, he reflected. Might as well charge out of these rocks and make an all-out assault on the rims which hid the watching, scheming Apaches and go down fighting.

He heard a sudden gasp from one of the men lying watchfully some little distance from him and Travis Eade, next to him, said: 'What's shaping up now?'

A movement of swirling dust out on the flats of the wilderness brought the Southerners and the bluecoats edging closer to the protecting rocks, squinting through the heat-charged air, gripping weapons expectantly.

The swirl of dust became larger, darkened into two thick banners and became two horsemen, riding furiously: men mounted on sprightly Indian mustangs, crouching low with their long, black hair streaming behind them as they approached the rocks. They were Apaches, but they came not from the rim-rocks wherein Quino and his braves watched and waited, but off the wider reaches of the desert.

Travis Eade stared at them for a long time, watching their outlines become more distinct as distance between them and the *tinaja* decreased. Sweat, the cold sweat of apprehension, trickled down from under Eade's hat-brim. The air was charged with the hot pungence of the sun beating off shale, rocks and cactus. There were muttered curses from among the watchful men and the foreboding flap of unclean wings sounded distinctly from high above as the pair of buzzards returned to the dried-out water hole to circle in the sky and wait their opportunity.

'One of those varmints has a man tied across his pony!' exclaimed spiky-whiskered Sergeant Haggerty. 'Yes, by blazes, he has a man!'

Eade had already seen the bulky bundle flopping across the back of one of the speedily travelling mustangs. He remembered that Givens had been wearing a scuffed brown jacket and a pair of faded blue trousers when he rode out of here last night. Unless the heat was playing tricks with his eyes, the human being draped over the mustang's back, jouncing helplessly with every movement of the animal, was Givens.

Sergeant Abner Mapes put the realization that was in Eade's mind into words. From where he cradled his Spencer behind a gnarled rock, he said in a curiously flat voice, edged with a note of disbelief, 'That's Givens, they've got there! They must have caught him on the desert!'

'Of course they must,' snorted Clay Forrest. 'We

all heard the sound of ponies takin' off after Hertz an' Givens left last night. None of us dared talk about it, but now we know what those damned varmints have done. They caught up with Hertz an' Givens!'

'I don't see Hertz,' murmured one of the California Column troopers. 'That's Givens, all right, but I don't see Hertz.'

Eade had his carbine to his shoulder, sighting the head of one of the approaching Apaches. The Indian was just out of easy range. Eade lowered the rifle. He was curious as to what was developing with this move from the Apaches. There would be little point in shooting just now.

He saw the pony-riding savages halt with a slithering of hoofs and the one who carried Givens' body across his mount heft the civilian coachman's form out of its position and drop it down to the dust. Then, he saw Givens kick and thresh desperately at the feet of the pony as if to give a graphic demonstration to those in the watersink that he was not dead.

'He ain't dead!' breathed Ben Forman. 'They got him trussed up, but he's still alive!'

The pair of desert warriors sat their mounts, just out of carbine range, holding a brief pose in which they seemed to be two defiant statues. Then, the one who had been unburdened by Givens' trussed-up bulk, showed that he carried a trophy, too. Slowly, he raised something in the air,, something of a vaguely blue colour which he flourished high and waved in the sunlight. A bright, brassy flash was struck from its metal trappings.

It was a Union cavalry forage cap.

The Indian waved it at the rock cluster, making

an elaborate ceremony of the gesture, then he flung it disdainfully to the floor of the desert.

'So they got Hertz,' rumbled Haggerty. 'That damned ace of spades didn't bring him any luck! They must have killed Hertz and left his body on the desert, but what are they doin' with Givens?'

Eade thought he knew the answer to that one and he framed it in colourless words, feeling a helpless fury rising in him as he spoke.

'It's all part of the cat-and-mouse game they're playing with us. I've seen Comanches do something like this in Texas. They trussed Givens up and put him just out of our reach. Unless I'm mistaken, there are wet rawhide strips tied around his head, his wrists and ankles. The rawhide will contract as it dries in the sun and we'll be forced to watch Given die in agony before our eyes. The Indians will position themselves out of range so we can't hit them, but they'll shower arrows into anyone who makes a dash towards Givens.'

He heard a short, shocked gasp at his back and turned to see Marguerite Norman crouching close to him. He had not known the girl had joined the defenders at the outer line of rocks. He saw that her colour had drained from under the sun-smitten cheeks, saw that she was shocked and looking as near to being scared as he had yet seen her.

'Can't we do anything for him?' she asked huskily. 'We can't see him die under torture like that!'

'The Indians know that,' said Eade. 'They know it's against our ethics to watch a man die that way and that one, or a couple of us, will be fool enough to run out and attempt to save him. Watch those savages and you'll see what I mean.'

Silently, they watched the two Indians turn their ponies' backs towards the water-sink and walk the animals in the direction of the rims for several yards. Then, they dismounted and squatted close to a scatter of weatherworn rocks.

Close to the far rims, banners of hoof-risen dust were rising. Looking like toys at this distance, moving steadily forward out of the sun-splashed rim-rocks in sedate single file, came a line of mounted Apaches. They were heading for the scatter of rocks where their brothers who had ventured after the desperately travelling white riders under cover of night had established themselves. They approached easily and with a fearsome dignity to their riding.

The whites watched the riders fan out into a long front, moving forward with savage pageantry and halting when they reached the line of rocks where the two who had dropped Givens' bound form and the forage cap of Corporal Hertz to the floor of the desert squatted. The mass of savages stood just out of carbine range; between them and the whites in the rock cluster, the feebly struggling Givens lay on the baking shale.

The Apaches made a flamboyant business of producing arrows and notching them into their bowstrings. They could not hit the rock cluster from their position any more than they could be hit by bullets fired by the besieged whites. Some dismounted and squatted on rocks, others remained on the backs of their motionless ponies. They looked as though they were prepared to stay in that position all day and Eade, Haggerty and others among the party in the rocks who had experience of Indian fighting knew they probably would.

Desert warrior and white man considered each other through the distorting heat-veils and, in the centre of the arena between them, lay the bait that would, so the Indians hoped, bring at least one white out of hiding to face death: the helplessly bound, tortured Givens.

It was the beginning of a war of nerves in which the Apaches held most of the advantages.

NINE

It was, to Marguerite Norman, a long, strained period which had the quality of being outside space and time; a waiting period in which terror might be loosed against them in the space of a heart-beat. A heat-charged, tensed and unreal time of apprehension.

Out on the desert lay Givens. When Marguerite looked through the interstices between the rocks and cactus which formed their barrier against the desert and the Apaches, she could see that the man who had been captured by the savages and placed there in the pounding, remorseless sun had indeed been treated as Eade had said. The thongs of wet rawhide tied about his forehead and ankles were plainly visible. His hands were fastened behind his back, but the girl knew his wrists would be bound by wet rawhide too. She had heard of this Indian torture before. It was, like most aspects of desert-dweller culture, extremely simple. And it was extremely efficient. As the green hide dried in the heat, it contracted, cutting into the flesh of the victim and causing terrible, fiery agonies.

Marguerite considered the writhing form of

Givens out there in the tract of wilderness between
their rock cluster and the steady, motionless line of
stony faced Apaches who were waiting . . . just waiting. She burned with an almost crazy desire to run
out and help the tortured man, but she knew that
was what the Indians wanted. They were waiting
their opportunity to shower a storm of arrows at
whoever ventured first from the water-hole to aid
the tortured man.

For the first time, Marguerite Norman came close
to losing her nerve. She had been prepared for death
ever since that first fight with the Apaches in which
the whites had beaten them out of the cluster of
rocks. For the last several hours, she had felt that
death was certain and had placed a blanket of self-
deception over the prospect. It would come swiftly
and then it would be over. There was a part of her
mind which insisted that death did not come swiftly
for a white woman when she fell into the hands of
these desert Indians whose very name meant
enemy, but she shook off this insistence.

She had not thought of the preliminaries to death
at which the Apaches were so ingenious. She was
witnessing one now.

Those Indians, some standing, others squatting
and still others astride their mustangs, waiting out
yonder in a straight and rock steady line, looked
impassive, cruel and, somehow, as enduring and
ageless and as totally indestructible as the rearing
rims and spiny mesas of this sprawling, oven-hot
wasteland. They were part of this land, as much
carved out of rock and shaped from harsh shale as
the land itself, as cruel and savage as the other
living things produced by the desert: the cactus, the

catclaw, the barbed Spanish dagger, the rattlers, the
winging, watching carrion-seeking buzzards.

They would kill the whites, but they would kill as
the desert killed – by thirst, snake-bite or poison
barb. They would kill slowly.

The thought built itself up within Marguerite's
mind: it became a magnified nightmare. These men
with whom she was caught in the tangle of rocks
were as helpless against the might of the Apaches as
a kitten would be against a lion. She considered
them: the band of stubble-faced, ragged men who
had called themselves prospectors but who had
more or less admitted to be ex-secessionist soldiers,
led by the tall, scar-faced, curiously silent and reflective man whom the younger man with the injured
shoulder had referred to as 'Major'; the horse-
soldiers from Fort McDowell under their fierce-
bearded sergeant and the remaining civilian coachman, an ageing, sun-seamed man whose name she
did not even know. They seemed good enough men,
brave enough and tough enough to fight for their
lives until the bitter end. And she knew it would be
a bitter end, for the whites, for all their toughness
and their determination to tame a land such as this,
were doomed. They could not fight the desert and
the things of the desert and emerge victorious. The
desert would wear them down and the men carved
and moulded, shaped, hardened, edged and
tempered by the desert would kill them!

Marguerite remembered that an unseen barrier
had been set up between the bluecoats and the
desert-punished 'prospectors' all of whom spoke like
Southerners. It was because of the war, she imagined. She remembered that some sort of personal

feud was shaping between Eade and the one with
the full face and heavy moustache, the man they
called Forrest. A clash of personalities, she imagined, something she could not understand but something which was a definite, grinding difference
between the 'prospectors'. How petty and meaning-
less it all was, she thought. The war between North
and South meant nothing out here in the tortured
wilderness and what was the value of a quarrel
between the so-called 'prospectors' in the face of the
death that was about to come to them? The desert
was about to kill them, about to settle all differences
beween them, and the granite-faced agents of death,
the men created by the desert, waited . . . waited . . .
waited. . . .

Marguerite Norman made an attempt to force
down the nightmarish apprehension. She would put
thoughts of impending destruction out of her mind
by doing what she had done so frequently during
these past hours: giving her attention to the youngster with the injured shoulder, Dan Clyman.

The girl had been crouching amid the rocks and
cactus, looking out to the heat-danced point where
Givens lay trussed and feebly struggling in his
agony, backed by the Indians. As the hanging
tension of the situation preyed upon her mind and
pulled her nerves close to the point of breaking, she
had been unaware of the buzz of consultation
between the men. They all had their heads
together, bluecoat trooper and ex-Rebel, with Eade,
Forrest and Haggerty doing most of the hushed-
toned talking. With the determination to go down
to the wagon in which the injured Clyman lay,
Marguerite moved away from them and went

towards the lip of the dust-invaded sink. She stopped and gave a cry of protest as she saw young Dan Clyman coming up from the sink, walking with difficulty and clutching the Navy Colt Travis Eade had given him.

The young man's face was drawn and pale and his eyes were burning. The action of walking was obviously painful to his crushed shoulder in its improvized support, but he was heading towards the defenders in the rocks and cactus with a tight-lipped doggedness.

'Go back to the wagon,' Marguerite ordered. 'You're in no shape to be up here!'

'I'm all right,' Clyman said. 'There's somethin' about to bust loose – I can feel it in the way things have gone quiet – I'm gettin' in on the fightin' when it comes. If I sit in that wagon an' watch them buzzards float around much longer, I'll go crazy!'

He brushed past the girl and made his way towards Eade, Forrest and the rest, holding their hushed discussion.

Eade turned his head when he beard Clyman's approach and said harshly: 'Get back to the wagon! I told you to stay there!'

'To hell with the wagon an' all that's in it,' rasped the youngster. 'I'm fit enough to fight now!'

Eade, Clay Forrest and the remainder of the Confederates watched without comment as the young Texan crouched painfully behind a rock and looked out into the arena before the *tinaja* wherein the bait lay and at the far edge of which the Apaches waited motionless for the whites to emerge.

Clyman took in the scene for a long time then said: 'So they got one of these Yankees an' gave him the wet rawhide treatment. One of us will have to go out to him.'

'That's what the Indians figure,' stated Haggerty. 'That's why they're waitin' – to have themselves a little sport.'

'Can't hole up here an' see a man tortured that way,' protested Dan Clyman. 'I'm the one that can be dispensed with in this fix – I'm a burden on you other fellows, so I figure I'll go out an' try to help him.'

'You'll be killed,' protested one of the California Column troopers. 'Them 'Paches will make a pincushion of you!'

'I know it. But I figure I can be dispensed with. If I make a run out there with a knife an' this six-shooter, I might be able to cut that fellow's wrists loose and give him the gun before they finish me off. Then, at least, he'll have a chance of shootin' his way free!' The young Confederate corporal's plan was wild and feverish, but there was an expression of downright Rebel determination on his face as he put it into words.

'You'll never make it, kid,' pointed out Clay Forrest with a touch of gentleness in his voice which none of the Confederates had ever heard in it before. 'You can't run for one thing.'

'And we have another plan, for a second thing,' pointed out Travis Eade. 'We figure we might get Givens back here with a little military strategy – and I'm the one that'll go out there!'

Marguerite Norman, who had been watching the men restrain Dan Clyman in his crazy scheme, heard Eade outline a plan of action which they had decided upon during their hushed conversation. It seemed a long chance, but it had an element of thought and calculation in it which might just make it successful.

Eade proposed that a party of whites should venture out of the rocks with Spencer carbines, running forward to bring themselves within range of the waiting Apaches, and, putting their faith in the fact that the fire-power of the repeating carbines was greater than the range of the savages' arrows, fire a volley at the Indians. In the resultant confusion. Eade would rush forward and attempt to free Givens and a second volley would be fired into the Indian party to prevent them rushing at Eade on ponyback.

The remaining defenders at the water-hole would be waiting to fire on the Apaches if they rushed forward into range of their weapons as Eade worked at freeing the captured man. Everything in the scheme depended upon their keeping the Indians from shooting arrows on Eade and Givens and from making a mustang charge upon them as Eade tried to release the man who was tied down in the dust. Everything depended on a calculated use of the weapons of the white men against the primitive ones of the desert warriors.

Marguerite Norman watched the venturesome party making its preparations. Sergeant Haggerty and two of his troopers were going out with Eade and three of the 'prospectors' – they were Forman, Wain and Tucker, but she did not know their names – while the rest of the troopers, the remaining coachman, Forrest, Mapes and the injured Clyman settled themselves with ready carbines in the rocks as the final line of fire to hold back a too ambitious

charge from the lined-up Indians. She saw Eade
exchange his carbine for the Navy Colt he had
earlier given to Clyman and watched him produce a
Bowie knife with a wicked looking blade from a
sheath at his belt. He considered its edge for a
moment then pushed it back into its sheath. She
heard Sergeant Haggerty murmur something to one
of his troopers, remaining to defend the *tinaja*,
about taking care of the girl if things went badly
and, for the first time, realized that these men were
prepared to shoot her if it was apparent that she
was going to fall into Indian hands.

There was something in the thought that sent a
flame of anger rising in her. She could see that, as
commander of the party of soldiers charged with
protecting the coach, Haggerty was solicitous for her
safety and the sergeant knew all the vivid details of
the butchery of the passengers in the coach out of
Prescott which had been jumped by Apaches. He did
not want the girl to suffer, but she had an objection
to being regarded as a burden which would have to
be jettisoned when the going became too hazardous.

She strode forward towards Eade and Flaggerty
producing the small Derringer from the pocket of
her dress as she went, telling herself that she would
show these men she was not to be regarded as a sick
kitten to be disposed of quickly when chances of
survival seemed slight.

The sergeant stepped into her path and asked
abruptly: 'Where are you goin', ma'am?'

'To join those men in the rocks. If we're going to
hold the Indians back from making a rush at Mr
Eade we'll need everyone who can squeeze a trigger
firing from here, won't we?' Her sun-touched face

was clouded with anger but there was no hysteria in her quiet voice. She saw the sun-blackened face of Eade with its bullet-bite showing livid, regarding her over the sergeant's shoulder. The man from the South, the man she believed to be an ex-Confederate major, had a laughing light in his eyes. It sent the flame of anger leaping higher within her. He nodded towards the elegant little pistol she flourished.

'You aim to hold them off with that gambling man's firecracker?' he asked amusedly.

Marguerite Norman considered the Derringer and realized how ineffective it would be over a long range. She snorted with indignation and put the Derringer back into her pocket.

'I've never handled a carbine before, but I'll try if you give me one,' she said. 'I will not be left to stand around as a piece of spare baggage while the fighting is going on.'

'Isn't much to handling a Spencer,' said Haggerty. 'Pick one up an' one of my men will show you how to use it.'

The girl was lying in the line of defenders, sprawled among the rocks, with a Spencer at her shoulder as Eade and Haggerty gathered their men behind a gnarled boulder, preparing to make the desperate dash out into the open where a man waited to be rescued . . . and the Apaches waited to kill.

TEN

In the line of watching, waiting Apaches, a warrior whooped a ragged warning scream as the small party of whites charged out of the fringe of the besieged waterhole. In a shimmering instant, there were two surges of action so rapid that the defenders of the *tinaja* scarcely had time to take them in.

From the Indians, there was a speedy starting forward of mustangs the moment the whites ran out of the rocks. From the whites, there was a furious run out of the rocks for several yards to bring them forward to a point where their carbines would be effective among the Apaches. Running on a broad front, each man well spaced from the next, they churned desert dust like loping demons. Then they were down and the carbines were singing forth a crackling blast which slammed across the heat-charged air and staggered the Apache charge by sending several Indians falling from their steeds and making a wounded threshing mustang into a stumbling block for the others.

Eade, carrying only the Navy Colt, was up out of the dust the instant the first volley had its brief effect among the Indians. He put his legs to pounding like pistons and went haring in the direction of the trussed-up Givens. He crouched as he ran, trying to make himself as small as possible, aware that every step he took brought him closer to the range of the Apaches' arrows. He saw the tangle of Apaches at his front righting themselves and coming onward with a wild screeching. It seemed an eternity before the whites who lay in the dust at his back fired a second volley, taking care not to catch Eade in the cross-fire. The volley slammed into the advancing Indians, halted them for another brief instant during which more yelling warriors fell to the dust . . . then they continued their charge.

Eade, running at a crouch, saw the mounted braves as through a dim mist; yells sounded high in his ears and the crackle of carbines snarled again and again behind him. The fight was acted out around him as though it were a dream in which Eade had no part. He willed his legs to keep running towards Givens. He clutched the Bowie knife and the Colt in hands clammy with cold sweat. He had the hazy impression that he had lost his hat somewhere in the wild progression towards the tied and tortured coach-wrangler . . . but he held on to the weapons for dear life.

His heart sunk within him as he neared Givens. Through the dust and the noisy turmoil of the fight, there seemed to beat a persistent theme song which told Eade he had set himself a task which was doomed to failure. For Givens lay ahead of the mechanically running Texan – utterly motionless.

For a instant, he thought the captive was dead, that he had either succumbed to the treatment of

the desert warriors or had been killed by their
arrows, but he saw the trussed man move slightly.
He saw, too, that an arrow was protruding from
Givens' body and the sight caused him to blaze a
couple of random shots at the howling mass of
charging Apaches.

Eade reached Givens and fell into the dust beside
him. It was then that the action began to focus itself,
to have some reality for him. It was then that he
realized that the Indians were not charging, but
milling around in a tangled frenzy, those at the front
turning their mustangs' heads about in a panicky
effort to make a retreat and colliding with the
warriors behind them in the process. They were
trying to retreat from a slashing snarl of continuous
fire which came from behind Eade's back and which
must have been made by forces superior to the small
armed party which had covered the Texan's sprint
and the little party which defended the water-hole
combined.

Eade fought down the temptation to look back. He
concentrated on Givens. It was sufficient to know
that he had hitherto been the victim of a distortion
of sight and sound which he had known at other
times in battle: what had seemed to be an all-out
Indian charge which could only be victorious for the
savages was, in fact, the beginnings of a mad rout.

There was a crackling hail of cross-fire flying over
his head as he sprawled in the dust alongside
Givens. He saw that Givens was still breathing and
that the arrow was merely in his upper arm, probably having cut an artery to judge by the amount of
quickly flowing blood staining the coachman's
sleeve. Rawhide thongs about Givens's head had

bitten deep into the flesh, but Givens seemed to be fully conscious.

'Go back!' he croaked in a dry, tortured voice. 'Leave me here. I'm finished!'

'You're not finished,' Eade snorted, dashing dust and sweat out of his eyes with the back of his hand. Keeping his head low to avoid the continuous hail of musketry fire whizzing at the retreating Apaches, he turned Givens partially over to cut the rawhide strips binding his wrists with the Bowie knife. Givens moaned and complained of the pain in the arm in which the Apache arrow had hit him. Eade considered the rapidly spreading stain of blood on the sleeve and realized that he must give his immediate attention to stemming the flow.

The fight stormed around him with bullets biting into the now largely unmounted mass of desert braves while bold spirits among the Apaches tried to hold a firm front and pitch arrows at the whites. Eade saw a partially buried, sun-split boulder some yards away. If he could drag Givens behind it, it would offer some shelter from the tearing exchange of bullets and arrows in which he and the stricken man were caught. He bolstered the Navy Colt, thrust the Bowie knife into the sheath at his belt, took a grip under Givens' armpits and determinedly hauled the man, whose ankles were still bound together, in the direction of the boulder.

It was an aching, desperate struggle, with Travis Eade crouching low and making a slow backward progress.

He reached the boulder, flopped behind it and propped Givens against its weather eroded surface. From the lee of the boulder, he saw for the first time the forces that were pouring relentless defeat upon Quino's Apaches: Yankee soldiers!

Dozens of them, it seemed.

Vaguely, Travis Eade remembered that he had lately wished he could see a charge of those blue-coated riders against whom he had battled when he followed Stonewall Jackson. Now, it seemed, that the half-remembered wish had become reality. There were blue clad horse soldiers, holding a steady line over by the water-hole and driving the Apaches back with a hail of lead. To Eade, they appeared as phantoms in the fog of dust and powdersmoke, but they were real enough, as the effect of their fire on Quino's warriors proved.

Eade turned his attention and energies to Givens. The arrow in his arm was the cause of a rapidly gushing flow of arterial blood and the Southerner realized that he would have to devise a speedy means of halting the issue. Crouching behind the rock, he tore off his faded and ragged jacket and wrenched his coarse shirt from his back. Now stripped to the waist, he set to work on the stricken coachman as the din of battle and the sting of powdersmoke and dust whirled dizzily around him. He had no time to attempt to remove the arrow but he wrenched a broad strip from the sleeve of his shirt and made a tourniquet which he fastened around the coach-wrangler's upper arm. Recalling the knowledge of emergency wound dressing learned in the war, he fastened the arm against Givens' body, using the rest of the shirt as a soft pad under the armpit.

No sooner had he finished tying the final knot of the dressing than Givens gave a feeble cry of warn-

ing and Eade was aware of two streaking Indian
shapes whirling upon him from behind the rock.
They came with such speed that Eade was caught
with neither Bowie knife nor Colt in his hands, but
he had an oddly lingering view of the faces of the
savages as the pair bore down upon him: he saw
their dark features twisted into grimaces of hatred.
He had a hazy view of stone-headed tomahawks
raised high as the Apaches closed with him and the
last detail he remembered as he ducked to escape a
whistling swipe from one of the tomahawks was
that one of the Apaches – a squat individual with
crazy fire in his eyes – was wearing a sun-faded
Yankee army tunic with the tarnished chevrons of a
corporal still intact.

The blow of the tomahawk missed Eade and the
Southerner twisted his body into a leaping dance
and grabbed the Apache's descending arm with both
hands, hauling the savage downwards with all the
force he could muster. Savage and Texan fell into the
hot shale in a snorting tangle and, as Eade went
down, he heard the bellowing cough of a revolver,
almost in his ear, it seemed, and the report was
followed by a bubbling scream.

The Apache had dropped the tomahawk as Eade
had yanked him down. He rolled on the white man,
crushing him down into the harsh surface of the
desert. Eade could smell the pungent grease with
which the desert warrior's black hair was plastered
and the world, with its cacophony of battle noises,
began to grow dim, floating away into tear-hazed
mists as the savage began to throttle him.

Somehow, Eade's hand contacted the handle of the
dropped tomahawk. The feel of it brought Eade's

waning consciousness back to a brief moment of reality. It was sufficient time for him to grip the Indian
weapon with all his might and swing it up from the
ground in an arc which brought the blade crashing
into the spine of the brave who lay on top of him. The
Apache released his grip about Eade's neck at once
with a throaty gasp of anguish. Eade brought his
knees up into the Indian's abdomen sharply and put
all his ebbing strength into forcing the savage's
weight from him. The Apache, still struggling, yielded
and their positions were reversed, Eade rolling the
desert warrior into the dust. Clawing and snarling,
the Apache tried to hold off the Texan, but Eade
pinned him down with one hand about his neck,
raised himself to a kneeling position then crashed the
flat of the tomahawk blade against his skull.

He came up from the dead Indian, spitting dust
and brandishing the tomahawk in readiness to deal
with further savages. But, as his vision cleared and
he became aware of his surroundings, he saw that
there were no more Apaches in the immediate vicin-
ity. The warriors had made a wild and complete
retreat into the wilderness, leaving a trail of
huddled braves and mustangs in their wake.

There were men surging around him, men in the
natty. short jackets of US cavalrymen, and the
tattered, sun blackened men of Eade's own stamp:
Forrest, Wain, Forman, Mapes and Tucker. Givens
was still propped against the rock. He was holding
Eade's Navy Colt in his hand and there was a drib-
ble of smoke emerging from its mouth.

The coach-wrangler grinned at Eade and
motioned with the weapon to the Indian in the faded
cavalry tunic, sprawled in death beside the savage

the Texan had killed.

'I managed to grab up this gun an' lessen the odds when them varmints showed up,' he announced. Eade remembered the bellow of the Colt and the dying screech of the Apache as he had battled with the second one.

A voice said: 'Sure was some fight while it lasted an' I guess we've seen the last of this bunch. That dead one in the old cavalry tunic is Quino himself!'

Eade shook his head like a wet terrier and goggled at the man who had imparted this information. He was a lean, hatless Yankee corporal whose face was powder blackened but brightened by a wide grin. He was Hertz, whom the defenders of the water-hole imagined to be dead.

'I thought the 'Paches got you out on the desert,' Eade said dully.

'They darned near did,' affirmed the card-playing corporal, 'but this was one time in my life when the ace of spades turned up lucky. I guess that's what comes of having a lady choose the cards.'

'Guess it is,' said a soft voice beside the corporal.

They turned to see Marguerite Norman there. Powder had darkened the delicate face framed in the poke bonnet and she still clutched her Spencer carbine. 'You had yourself quite a battle, Major Eade,' the girl commented. 'These gentlemen in blue were cheering you.'

'You look as though you did pretty well yourself,' Eade praised. 'Did you use that Spencer?'

Marguerite Norman nodded. 'I didn't like the idea of using it, but convinced myself that there was no point in escaping from the war in Mexico only to die in this fight – so I used it.'

'She used it well, too,' observed Sergeant Haggerty. 'Never seen a woman with such fight in her.' The sergeant had obtained a cigar from one of the relieving force of troopers. He thrust it into his hair-fringed mouth and activated his flint-and-wheel lighter. 'Sure was thoughtful of these soldiers to bring along some of the finer things of life when they came to our aid,' remarked the California Column non com. through clouds of smoke. Eade sniffed, noted that the cigar was of the pungent quality which Haggerty appeared to relish and offered no comment.

'How did these troops come to be here?' Eade asked.

'Hertz brought 'em. 'Pache scouts went after them an' there was a fight in the darkness. Hertz an' Givens got separated an' Hertz heard Givens yell that he was overpowered an' Hertz should go ahead without him. Hertz was lucky enough to fight his way clear, but he lost his forage cap. The 'Paches must have picked it up as a trophy, which made us believe they'd killed Hertz.'

'So Hertz reached Fort McDowell and brought cavalry,' mused Eade.

'And the cavalry ensured our future,' said Haggerty on a stream of cigar smoke.

The observation brought Eade sharply back to a consideration of what the future would hold for the ex-Confederates and himself.

ELEVEN

They rested for an hour at the *tinaja*. Casualties among the whites were slight: a couple of the relieving body of Fort McDowell cavalry had suffered flesh wounds from chance Apache arrows, Abner Mapes had had the lobe of an ear nicked by a stray bullet and had some lurid opinions to express concerning the marksmanship of Yankees. Givens, weakened but in no serious condition, had the benefit of more expert attention than Eade had been able to give him from the young captain who had commanded the relieving body of Fort McDowell cavalry, a student of surgery before he joined the California Column.

During the rest at the water-hole, the barriers between Yankee and Confederate which had fallen in the fury of their stand against Quino's braves began to be subtly erected once more. Eade and his weary companions sat at one side of the scatter of rocks and cactus; Haggerty and his men were mixing with the other bluecoats who had come from the fort. The young Yankee captain was a little apart from them, attending to Givens and looking at Dan

Clyman's shoulder, with Marguerite Norman assisting.

Captain Clay Forrest, his fleshy face blackened by powdersmoke, sat on a rock close to Eade, drinking tepid water from a canteen. Forrest, like all those besieged at the dried-out sink, had fought well against the Apaches. Now, in company with the remainder of the defenders, he found time to slake his burning thirst and wash the gritty dust and taste of powder from his mouth. But other things than thirst burned within Clay Forrest. He edged closer to Eade when he had finished drinking and came to the point at once. He nodded towards the back of the young cavalry captain: 'What do you figure to do about him an' that gold?' he asked. 'Pretty soon that captain will get through lookin' at their injuries an' he'll start askin' questions. Even if he don't come enquirin' for himself, Haggerty or one of the other bluebellies will tell him we're Rebs, then they'll take us as prisoners an' haul us to McDowell to be hanged!'

'Nobody' goin' to hang me,' put in Abner Mapes, surly-faced in the background. 'Nobody will string me up just because I fought for states' rights!'

'That's the way we all feel!' confirmed Ben Forman.

The Rebels shifted their sprawling, weary bodies into a mass behind Forrest as if symbolic of their taking a solid stand behind his leadership. Eade had known that this moment would come. The matter of how he should behave as the commander of a force which carried Confederate gold now that the war was over had nagged at him persistently since Marguerite Norman had shown him the newspaper

with the news of the collapse of the Rebel government. He was now sagging with a desperate weariness, all his energy seeming to have drained from
his frame during the fight on the desert. He was in
poor shape for thinking clearly and making deci-
sions, but this block of gaunt-faced men with their
questioning, near-hostile eyes demanded an answer.

In their minds, the end of the war was the lip of
a great cavity. Beyond that cavity yawned an
unknown future. They could not conceive of the
Yankees being merciful in victory – especially if it
were true that Abraham Lincoln had been assassi-
nated by a Southern sympathizer. With Washington
government men such as Stanton, Seward and
Chase – haters of the Confederate cause, all of them
– in command of affairs, they felt sure that every
Johnny Rebel would be severely punished for his
part in what the Yankees called 'the great rebellion'.

Eade's mind took a different turn. The South
might be vanquished, he thought, but someone
would have to rebuild the South. The South would
require men of courage and determination if it was
to create an honourable future out of the ashes of
war. There was no disgrace in an honourable surrender and, if the noble Virginian, Robert E. Lee had
surrendered to Grant, then there was no point in a
handful of obscure Rebels attempting to hold out.
The sensible thing to do, as an officer of Lee's army,
would be to follow the chief's lead and surrender
with dignity, then try to work for recovery of the
Southland. Eade saw that vivid picture of Pickett's
charge up that slope of Cemetery Ridge at
Gettysburg once more. Perhaps Lee, too, had realized how much of the South died on that last

tremendous wave which broke upon the rock of the
Union at Gettysburg. Perhaps Lee, too, had been
haunted by it for two years, as Eade had. There
must be many other nightmares of a similar kind to
keep old Bobby Lee awake when the grey bearded
warrior was out of the saddle long enough to rest his
rheumaticky bones in a bed.

Yes, an honourable surrender was preferable to
seeing more young men of the South splintering
before Yankee guns and someone must work for
those the dead had left behind: the wives, the children and the mothers of the Confederacy.

To put this into words for the men before him was
going to be difficult for Eade, but he had spoken
briefly with the young commander of the relieving
column roused by Corporal Hertz. He had asked the
captain about news from the capital and how the
post-war turmoil was being settled. The young officer, not knowing that he was speaking to an ex-
Confederate, had told him what the latest papers to
reach Fort McDowell had contained and had added
a piece of information which gave him hope in the
mercy of the Union. On this, his determination to
return to the South was founded. It would have to be
put to his men and the time was now.

'Boys, I've already spoken with that captain,' he
began solemnly. 'He told me something which makes
me believe that we can ride back out of this wilderness without fear of punishment. He said that he'd
lately received a paper from the East in which the
full report of Lee's surrender was given. The terms
were simply that every secesh soldier lays down his
arms and promises not to fight the Union again –
there's no suggestion of hanging. It seems that when

Bobby Lee and Grant met at this Appomattox place, Lee explained that all the horses of his cavalrymen were their own property and he wondered if the farm boys in his army could ride home as soon as possible because they'd be just in time to do a little spring planting. And Grant said that would be all right. Seems he said there was no point in men hanging around when they could be home and working their farms into shape.'

There was a heavy silence among the men, then Charlie Tucker, a farmer himself in the days of peace, asked huskily: 'He said that? Old US Grant, the same one that took Vicksburg, didn't raise a yell for the lives of Rebel traitors?'

'It seems not,' answered Eade. 'I gather he and Lee sat around for a long time talking over old times – they soldiered together in Mexico back in '46.'

The men considered the point for a moment, then Clay Forrest raised a scornful objection.

'I don't believe a word of it! The Yankees ain't goin' to let this thing settle down so easy – they're plenty vindictive an' they'd want to avenge Lincoln's death. The stuff that captain told you is just Yankee lies!' Forrest's eyes considered Eade with a calculated insolence. Animosity towards the Texas major which Forrest had kept long hidden was beginning to reveal itself. In the lull after the battle, Forrest had revived the earlier clash of personalities between himself and Eade. This time, the watching men felt it might be fanned into an outright fistfight as they saw the reaction worked in Travis Eade's face when the captain from Missouri pushed the argument further.

'What are you goin' to suggest, Eade – that we

knuckle down to these Yanks an' surrender ourselves and the gold to them?' Forrest demanded. As he spoke, he raised himself from the rock on which he had been seated and he towered over Eade, spraddle-legged and with his fists knotted. 'Is that what you're goin' to order us to do? If you are – I ain't doin' it!'

Travis Eade felt a thundering anger rise within him. Energy seemed to come coursing back into his body and he stood up abruptly, stepped up to Forrest and stood almost nose-to-nose with him. When Eade spoke, his words came whistling through half-clenched teeth.

'I'll remind you that I'm in command of this task force, Captain,' he said. 'It's for me to decide what I'll do. If the rest of the Confederacy has surrendered itself and all its arms and stores, then I have no option than to hand over my command and everything I hold – and that includes the bullion!'

Eade saw Forrest's face register disgust and was aware of the scowling hostility which darkened the faces of the party of Confederates squatting behind the captain.

'You won't hand me over to any damyanks to be strung up,' stated Forrest in a harsh growl. 'If you're a blasted coward who'll throw down his arms that easily, I ain't. There's bound to be someone who'll keep fightin' for the South an' who can use that bullion. Quantrill, Todd an' Anderson – I bet those three fellows haven't surrendered. They'll be fightin' somewhere an' I aim to join 'em with that bullion!'

'*Quantrill, Todd and Anderson!*' snarled Eade, spitting out the names distastefully. 'Didn't anyone ever tell you the Confederacy has disowned them?

The South fights with soldiers, not murdering brig-
ands. Didn't you hear about what Quantrill did to
the town of Lawrence? Didn't you hear about the
killing of unarmed civilians? Don't talk to me about
Quantrill, Todd and Anderson, or I'll push your teeth
down your throat!'

The men watched the little drama build towards
its climax in this secluded section of the rocks
surrounding the dried-up sink where the content
and vehemence of the harshly whispered argument
were hidden from the Yankees. Forrest glowered at
Eade, opening and closing his big hands in an angry
reaction. Bitter resentment shadowed the faces of
the four remaining Confederates. George Wain
stepped closer to the arguing officers and voiced a
sentiment which his companions shared.

'We ain't givin' ourselves up, Major. We didn't get
this far an' lose Dufay, Janniver an' Grover, just to
hand ourselves an' that bullion over to bluebellies.'
From the background came a murmur of assent.

Eade tried to put it to them on a sober, reasoning
basis without success.

'Look, this thing has to be done in a soldierly fashion,' he told them. 'If General Lee has surrendered
then that should be good enough for any
Confederate officer. The chief didn't hand over his
sword without realizing the South couldn't survive.'

'That's damned yellow defeatist talk!' protested
Charlie Tucker. 'The South can survive!'

Eade turned on him quickly. Words and senti-
ments that had been accruing within him since the
summer of '63 – that tragic summer for the
Confederate States – found their first outlet: 'I saw
Pickett's charge at Gettysburg, Tucker,' he growled.

'I saw the whole thing go down before those Yankees
– it was the slaughter of the vigorous young men of
the South. Have you seen what the Confederate
Army has in its ranks as its latest recruits? They're
senile old men and scared little boys! I saw them in
Richmond last year and I saw the way the citizens
were living – struggling along on miserable rations
so that the nation could attempt to feed its army. Do
you think the South could survive in that way: with
the Yankees blockading the coast, no cotton going
out and no revenue coming in? There's a time for
fighting and a time for surrender with honour, so
something can be salvaged from the wreck and
those who are still alive can do something for the
families of those who died!' Eade paused for a
moment, watched the faces of his men registering
varying emotions then added on a less harsh note:
'Besides, there's another matter. Young Clyman back
there is badly hurt. He fought those 'Paches mighty
gallantly, though he was in pain, and we owe him
the duty of taking him to Fort McDowell with the
rest of this party so he can be treated by a compe-
tent doctor.'

Forrest was still standing, legs a-straddle, inches
away from the Texan. Derision showed plainly on
his face.

'I see we've come back to that old argument,
Eade,' he observed on a low, drawling note. 'I figure
there's more in this than meets the eyes of simple
fellows such as these boys an' me. I don't believe you
have half so much concern for Dan Clyman as you
have for the Yankee woman. Oh, sure, we heard you
giggling down by the bed of the sink last night.
Seems to me you have such a strong desire to stick

around with these Yankees simply because of that
girl. . . .'

Travis Eade could never have explained what it
was in the Missouri captain's voice which caused
him to do it, but he threw a savage punch at Forrest
as the man was in mid-sentence. It hit Forrest's chin
with a meaty *thwack* and the captain was taken off
his feet by the piledriver blow of the Texan's craggy
fist. He scooted backwards, sending the remainder
of the party of Southerners dancing out of his path
as he whirled down to the shale and rocks to sprawl
full length there.

Forrest lay there for an instant, looking up into
the sunburnished azure of the desert sky. Then he
spat blood from his mouth, raised himself slowly,
crouched on all fours with all the brutality of the
Middle Border reflected in his eyes. He came up like
a spring, surging at Eade with his big fists flailing.

Travis Eade was waiting for him. He launched
himself straight at Forrest as the Missourian
pitched at him. They met in a headlong collision of
pounding blows, each standing almost toe-to-toe,
neither giving ground and the blows slamming with
tornado force.

A shot halted it. A sharp blast from a Colt's
revolver which sent a bullet snapping angrily over
the heads of the snarling, fighting men and froze
them in mid-action. The excited party of
Southerners froze, too, eyes turned towards the
point where the shot came from.

Captain Cowell, the smooth-cheeked young
commander of the detachment of Yankee horse-
soldiers which had come out to the wasteland on
Corporal Hertz's summons, stood there. He was

holding a pistol which dribbled smoke. Two of his cavalrymen stood behind him, holding Spencer carbines as if they meant business.

'We'll quit the fighting, gentlemen,' said Cowell tartly. 'Mauling each other like grizzly bears is most unbecoming behaviour for officers – General Lee and the late General Jackson would never approve. You might as well know that my men and I have been standing behind one of these rocks for the last ten minutes. We've heard every word you said about your being Southern soldiers and about the bullion you have in your wagon. I'm asking for your formal surrender, then you can come back with me to Fort McDowell to make it official and take the oath of allegiance to the United States!'

TWELVE

Captain Cowell stepped into the midst of the Confederates closely followed by his carbine wielding troopers. He was a pleasant faced young man who possessed a rather exaggerated degree of military correctness. Eade and Forrest had seen enough of him, however, to appreciate that he was no swaggering blusterer, as some young Northern officers were. He'd proved his ability in fighting off Quino and his warriors.

Cowell considered Eade and Forrest. They had a dusty and ragged appearance; both were weary and blood streamed from their noses. For all their sun-blackened, desert-hardened, appearance, thought the young Yankee, there was something about them at this moment which imparted the appearance of wilful small boys caught out at some misdemeanour. The four remaining members of the Confederate force stood about the erstwhile fistfighters with surly faces turned to the Fort McDowell officer and his troopers.

The Union officer holstered his Colt, leaving the party covered by the troopers. He considered Eade and Forrest with a disapproving eye.

'There's been something of a conspiracy of silence between Sergeant Haggerty and his men,' he told them. 'They have not seen fit to tell me that you are – or were – secessionist soldiers still under arms. No doubt they have such a high opinion of the way you conducted yourselves when you made common cause against the Apaches that they feel they owe you an opportunity to ride away from here without any unpleasantness. That's a most unmilitary attitude and I'm afraid I can't condone it, especially now that I know you are carrying a load of bullion, probably intended for the treasury of the Confederate States. Since the Confederacy is no more, I suppose I am justified in taking the gold in the name of the United States.'

'Don't make speeches, Captain. If Haggerty and his men didn't tell you we're secesh. who did?' rumbled Forrest, somewhat chastened at learning of the silence of Haggerty and his men.

'I heard Miss Norman refer to Eade as "Major" Eade, then I recalled that all of you 'prospectors' have Southern accents. When you began to question me about news from Washington, Eade, I suspected even more that you were secessionists – therefore I decided to watch you closely. What my men and I heard from behind that rock was enough to confirm my suspicions,' Cowell said. 'The terms of the surrender of the Confederacy require you to lay down your arms and take the oath of allegiance to the Union – that can be completed at Fort McDowell if you formally hand over your men and yourself, Major Eade. This is Indian country and I have a high regard for your fighting qualities, so I will not insist on your handing over your weapons before we reach the fort.'

The Rebels stood in a tight knot. In the face of this Yankee request for their surrender, all their earlier divisions seemed to have healed. The dusty air carried the busy sounds of the remainder of the soldiers preparing to take the horses and the Southerners' wagon out of the parched *tinaja*. Eade knew now that the final campaign of the war between the states had indeed been fought and that he and his men must conform to the surrender terms which the rest of the South had accepted. His feelings on the matter were mixed. He knew that any attempt to resist the demands of the Union would be as futile as the charge he had seen Pickett's men make on the slope of Cemetery Ridge at Gettysburg; he knew there would be a bitter campaign ahead in which the veterans of the Southern armies must fight for the peace-time integrity of the South. But, after the battles through which he had lived, after all the hopes which floated as high as the stars and bars of the determined lines of grey as they closed with the legions of blue, there seemed something totally unfitting in surrendering to a youthful Yankee captain of a volunteer Indian fighting outfit out in the wilderness far from the fields of glory and gore in Virginia, Maryland and Pennsylvania.

'Supposin' we don't feel inclined to surrender, Captain?' he asked Cowell.

The young Union officer shook his head slowly.

'I doubt if you'd be so foolish, Major. But, if you were misguided enough to imagine you could hold on to your arms and put up a fight, we would simply have to treat you as rebels under arms and shoot at you.'

Surprisingly, it was Clay Forrest who said: 'The captain's right, Major, an' guess we'll just have to admit defeat. His terms are generous enough – allowin' us to keep our arms in case of danger from the 'Paches. We're all in this situation together, as you once pointed out. I guess there can be no distinction between blue an' grey when you're all white folks out on the desert together. I figure there's nothing else for us to do but travel back to the fort with these Yankees an' hand ourselves over.'

The Missourian had an expression of extreme penitence on his face as he spoke. Eade felt there was something about it not quite genuine. Mapes, Tucker, Forman and Wain stood about with faces reflecting surprise at seeing the blustering captain, who had been so loud in his persistence that they attempt to fight on, knuckle under to the surrender terms so easily. Mingled emotions worked in them. To hand over their arms to the bluecoated enemy after the years of struggling against furious odds went against every particle of their fighting Johnny Rebel spirit; but it seemed that there would be no wholesale hanging of secessionists, that had been a mere phantasm conjured up by their exaggerated notion of the wickedness of the Yankee ogre. There was the thought of Grant allowing Southern soldiers to ride home without delay to get in some spring planting on their farmsteads ... there was the powerful, pulling thought of home. . . .

They heard Eade's Texas drawl declaring slowly: 'I guess your suggestion is the wisest, Captain. I hand over my men and myself to you and will complete the surrender with your superiors when we reach McDowell.'

*

The slow-moving column moved towards the Gila River country and Fort McDowell, crawling under the furious heat of the afternoon sun; a company of soldiers, the coach, the Confederates and their wagon. After the long term of inaction and the lack of water at the dried-out sink, most of the horses were weary and unable to make more than a labouring progress. Young Captain Cowell had suggested an overnight halt at a water-hole several miles ahead where the animals could be adequately refreshed and rested.

For the most part, Travis Eade's Confederates rode with a quiet acceptance of their fate. But anyone who paid close attention to Captain Clay Forrest would have noticed a certain rueful brooding in the eyes of the Southern officer who had, surprisingly, been so ready to accept the Union's surrender terms. Marguerite Norman rode in the coach in company with the injured Clyman and Givens, her thoughts occasionally turning to the men of the South who were to stack their arms at Fort McDowell.

Young Clyman had put up a stiff fight during the final mêlée with Quino's Apaches, in spite of his severely injured shoulder. He now seemed weak, white-faced and without energy. He was full of a youthful Texas fire and seemed to Marguerite to bear a dark resentment against Eade and Forrest for surrendering the task force to the Union. The girl and Givens had attempted to take the edge off the young corporal's grudge by talking of a new start for the South, but Dan Clyman continued in his gloominess.

'They shouldn't have surrendered us,' he complained. 'I'd rather have gone down fightin' you Yankees than suffer the disgrace of havin' to buckle under to the Union – then sneak home an' tell my folks I gave in.' He considered the dusty face of the girl who had given him devoted womanly care when he was racked by pain and tortured by delirium, and the oldster who bore the marks of Apache rawhide thongs about his forehead, a man who was even now sharing the last of his tobacco with the youthful Clyman. Clyman added quickly and sincerely: ' 'Course, I have nothin' against you people personally. All of you are mighty good people, not like other Yankees, I guess. But we were doin' our part in the war an' I figure we should have done it to the very end. "Surrender" ain't a word Texas men like – they wouldn't have it at The Alamo an' they've had little time for it ever since!'

'There's no sense in takin' that attitude, kid,' the coach-wrangler opined. 'There comes a time when you have to admit defeat an' take a different course in most folks' lives. General Lee could see there was no point in keepin' up with the bloodshed when the Rebel states were slowly bein' ground to pieces, an' he's a much older an' wiser man than you. Ain't no disgrace in givin' way to plain commonsense, an' that's just what Lee has done.'

'Besides, your people will probably be happy to see you return home alive and fit,' put in Marguerite Norman gently.

'It's the disgrace of it that I don't like,' grumbled Clyman. 'Bein' licked by the Yankees means we'll probably be ground down an' kicked around by you – not you personally, but by Stanton an' Seward an'

Chase an' all them big Yankees who'll be in power now that Lincoln is dead!'

'I doubt it,' comforted the Yankee girl. 'As I told Major Eade, President Lincoln said we are all one people again and the sooner we begin to see ourselves that way, the better it will be for us.'

Dan Clyman fell silent, reflecting on the point and listening to the rumble of the coach wheels and the jingle of trappings mingling with the plodding of weary hoofs.

Outside, Major Travis Eade rode slouched in his saddle, his hat brim casting an arc of shade on to his gloomily reflective face. Blood from the brief fight with Forrest had dried into a crust under his nose and bruises caused by the captain's sledging fists were beginning to darken on his dusty and stubbled face.

Around his horse jogged the men in blue and Sergeant Haggerty was nearby, polluting the desert air with another of the harsh stogies he liked to smoke. Behind him, rode Forrest and the remainder of the Confederate party, travelling under a cloak of brooding silence. In accordance with the agreement made with Captain Cowell, they still carried their arms against the appearance of more rampaging Apaches. But the spiny land, stretching its ragged breadth out on all sides, was silent under the hammering sun and, save for the occasional jackrabbit regarding the passing human beings from the scant shade of a saguaro cactus, there was no sign of life.

The jaded horses plodded the alkali-dusted trail with a determination that deepened as they scented the distant promise of water. The promise strengthened with every hoof-beat; the party made its tired progression through the broiling emptiness.

And they reached the rich water-hole as the red sun was lowering to the tangled peaks in the far west.

The place had a well-filled sink and harsh grass grew in abundance among the tumbled rocks at its edge. The party made camp, unhitched the animals and led them to the water's edge to drink. Later, when they had hauled the horses well away from the sink, to prevent them from indulging in the gluttony that would distend their bellies and sicken them after being so long without water, the motley bunch of men slaked their own thirsts.

They were close, now, to the Gila River and there were broken rimmed mountains over towards the east. The air had a freshness to it that hinted at the nearness of fertile land.

Travis Eade squatted at the water-hole, filling his cupped hands. As he did so, a sharp little breeze whipped through the rocks, tanning a peppering of dust across the now rippled surface of the water and cutting against the Texan's cheek with an unaccustomed coldness. Eade froze, the cup made by his hands raised halfway to his lips and water dripping in unheeded globules back into the sink.

There was a warning in that quick gust of wind. Eade had known such spirited breezes in Texas – and they heralded the howling, destructive 'blue northers' of that land.

Unless Eade was no Texan, there was a storm coming up.

It was dark. The party had bedded down among the

rocks at the *tinaja*, some huddled close to the ex-Confederate wagon, others near the coach. On Captain Cowell's orders, four cavalrymen squatted in the rocks at the rim of the water-hole. Quino was dead and his band probably dispersed without its leader, but the more powerful Cochise still rampaged in this country and the white who bedded down without posting sentries was begging for the Apaches to take advantage of him.

An occasional sharp breeze stirred eddying spurts of dust around the water-hole and Eade was sprawled on harsh sand a little apart from the rest of the Confederate party, disturbed thoughts keeping him from sleep. Captain Cowell's decision to make the return to Fort McDowell a slow and easy one with an overnight stop at the lush water-hole was a wise one, Eade considered, bearing in mind that the party's horses were mostly jaded because of the enforced, waterless sojourn at the dried-out sink. The two injured men, Clyman with his broken shoulder and Givens who was still weakened by the effects of exposure to the desert sun and the rawhide torture of the Apaches, were now comfortable and would not be harmed by another night on the desert.

The nagging uncertainties and hot-blooded differences which had brought disharmony to Eade's task force seemed largely to have healed. Forrest, the fire-eating, last ditch Rebel who had so surprisingly agreed to the Yankee surrender terms, even seemed to be without malice towards Eade for the fist-fight which had flared between them before Captain Cowell had intervened.

Nevertheless. there was a portent in the air more threatening than the promise of the coming storm and Eade sensed it strongly as, refreshed by water and strengthened by the army rations which Cowell's men had brought along, he sought a few hours of sleep. Fitful sleep came to him at last and he had no idea how long he had slept when he was wakened by an urgently shaking hand.

It was the hand of Marguerite Norman. She was sprawling in the shale beside him, gripping his arm and jarring him into consciousness. There was a sliver of moon riding through the high-piling storm-heads in the desert sky and it put a pale sheen on the girl's face framed in its poke bonnet. Her eyes were brightened by points of light which spoke of sudden fear and she whispered to Eade: 'Your men are making a move to run away with the gold. Captain Forrest is disarming Captain Cowell and the rest of the soldiers!'

The last remains of sleep fell from Travis Eade. He sat bolt upright.

'What do you mean? He can't do that – the odds are too great!'

'He's doing it,' Marguerite assured him. 'I was sleeping close to your wagon when I heard someone moving around. I heard voices. It was Forrest and some of the others. I heard Captain Forrest ask one of the men if he'd taken care of the sentries and the other said he and his companion had done it with ease. Then Forrest told two of them to go to where the horses are tethered and bring up a team to hitch to the wagon while he and the others disarmed Captain Cowell, Sergeant Haggerty and the remainder. They have Dan Clyman with them and that youngster is in no shape to go wandering off into the desert again.'

Cold fury swelled in Travis Eade. 'The blasted fools! They can't pull off a move like this – they're heading full tilt for disaster!' he growled, pitching the blanket to one side and starting to come to his feet.

'Can't we, Major?' inquired a mocking voice from the shadows. 'Can't we pull it off? It's been tolerably easy so far, only trouble was that no one thought of keepin' an eye on the Yankee lady an' she crawled among the rocks to warn you.'

Captain Clay Forrest stepped nearer, holding a Spencer carbine in a menacing manner. Eade and the girl could not see his face distinctly, but the fitful moon brightened the trappings he was wearing about his middle. He had strapped on two US Army belts, each heavy with a polished leather holster.

The wind was mounting. It scattered fine dust in the eyes of Eade, the girl and Forrest. Forrest spat irritating grains of it from his lips and continued talking: 'Takin' advantage of these Yankees wasn't so difficult. The sentries were so busy lookin' out towards the desert that they didn't hear Mapes, Wain, Tucker an' myself sneak up behind 'em. We just grabbed 'em around their necks an' now they're lyin' back in the rocks, quiet as mice, with their yellow neckerchiefs in their mouths an' their wrists tied to their ankles with their own belts. Yankees!' He made a noise which indicated utter scorn.

'What are you aiming to do?' asked Eade quietly. 'What the blazes do you imagine you can accomplish by a move like this?'

'Get clear of here while there's a chance an' get to Mexico with that gold, then ultimately find someone who's continuin' the South's fight.'

'Like Quantrill, Todd or Anderson?' asked Eade
disparagingly. 'You still following that crazy dream,
Forrest?'

'It's no dream,' growled Forrest. 'There's bound to
be some Rebel with some fight left in him. You heard
what those soldiers said earlier – that they'd heard
of Johnny Rebels scootin' for the border when they
heard of Lee's surrender. They ain't runnin' away,
Eade, just makin' sure they're on hand to fight
another day. An' that's what me an' the boys aim to
do. We're leavin' you, of course, you're such a Yankee
lover that we figure you'd be happier here!' The barb
in this observation was not wasted on Eade, nor on
the girl who stood at his side. It was tempered of the
same steel which had cut the tension between
Forrest and Eade earlier, setting them to pounding
each other with their knuckles.

Eade chose to let it ride on this occasion. Forrest
faced him with a Spencer at the ready and the
Confederate captain was in an ugly enough mood to
use it if provoked. The Texan began to wonder how
much of Forrest's determination to make a getaway
with the gold was due to his crazy desire to keep
fighting for the stars and bars and how much to
plain, unvarnished avarice. Whatever the motiva-
tion, the Missouri man's scheming had brought him
to this decisive juncture – and the remnants of the
Southern task force were backing him.

'You played it very smoothly, Forrest,' Eade
commented. 'You were quick enough to agree to
surrender only because you figured there'd come a
time when you'd be trusted enough and vigilance
would be slack enough for you to cut loose with the
bullion. And you talked the rest of the boys into it.

You mesmerized them, I suppose, with that wild talk about Wade Hampton or some other general – or even men not fit to be mentioned in the same breath as Wade Hampton. Quantrill or Todd or Bloody Bill Anderson, would be around somewhere ready to fight. You're playing a crazy game and it'll never pay off.'

'It's paid off so far,' sneered Clay Forrest. 'Take a look back in those rocks near the coach an' the wagon an' you'll see the whole kit an' caboodle of them Yankees. Captain Cowell, too, tied up with their own belts. Mapes, Forman, Tucker, Wain, young Clyman an' I did that, just by sneaking with our carbines while they slept. Lickin' Yanks is plumb easy – an' we'll get clear of this bunch. You can have the whole parcel of 'em since your fancy runs to Yankees!' The jibing barb was there again; Travis Eade held down all his flaring temper, checking himself from springing forward at the armed man. 'Ain't goin' to be any yellow-bellied surrender to the Yankees at Fort McDowell for us,' snorted Forrest with heavy derision.

'I surrendered to Cowell because I've been convinced that Lee has surrendered,' Travis Eade stated in a flinty voice. 'What Lee sees as commonsense I see the same way. Someone has to keep his head to help the South retain its stability and self-respect and you're asking these boys to go chasing off on a wild attempt to get to Mexico.'

That's enough of the high-flyin' talk,' Forrest said curtly. 'I ain't interested in surrender; I only pretended. I was playing for time.' He made a motion with the Spencer. Two figures – Mapes and Wain – came out of the shadow-ridden rocks.

'Tie up the major an' take his Colt an' Spencer,' Forrest ordered. 'You can tie the lady's wrists, too, then take 'em over to the wagon an' the coach where we have the rest of the damyanks trussed.'

'No hard feelin's, Major,' said Abner Mapes with a genuine ring in his voice. 'The boys an' me just figure the captain is right an' all our efforts should not go for naught with a meek an' mild surrender to these Yankees.' Mapes set about relieving Eade of his weapons and tied his wrists behind his back.

'The captain is talking nonsense, Sergeant. I don't know whether he's super-patriotic or just plain greedy for gold, but he's leading you boys into more trouble than a formal surrender and a return home to the corn-patch will bring you.'

'Quit that talk!' ordered Forrest and Eade suspected he was touching a tender spot when he mentioned greed for gold.

Wain tied Marguerite Norman's hands behind her back and the girl suffered him to do so in silence.

'We don't like treatin' you this way, bein' Southern gentlemen, Ma'am, but we have to take precautions – you might be so fired with enthusiasm for the Yankee cause that you'd pull that gamblin' man's firecracker of yours an' shoot one of us rebels under arms,' apologized Forrest mockingly. 'Mapes an' Wain, take these two to the rest of the bunch yonder, time's a-wastin'.'

Eade and Marguerite were prodded through the rocks to the fringe of the water-hole where the coach and the wagon with its load of bullion were halted. Two of the Rebels had hitched a team between the shafts of the wagon and, for some reason, had gathered the remainder of the horses into a bunch.

Around the wagon sat the whole of Captain Cowell's Yankee troop and the young officer himself, all tied with their belts and gagged with their dusty yellow neckerchiefs. The handful of Southerners had ably demonstrated that a man was at his most vulnerable when his weapons were laid aside and he was snoring, having placed his whole trust in a few sentries.

There was something in the sight that tickled Eade, in spite of the circumstances of Forrest's coup. Under other circumstances, he would have been delighted to see a bunch of Federals surprised by a handful of Johnny Rebels and subjected to this kind of indignity; but he and his men had made common cause with this particular bunch of bluecoats. They had fought Apaches together; the relieving column under the smooth-cheeked young captain had certainly saved the lives of all those holed up at the dried out sink during that last desperate closing with Quino's vindictive braves.

More. Travis Eade had agreed to surrender at Fort McDowell. He had given the word of a Confederate officer, a word that had been honoured and trusted by Captain Cowell who had allowed the party of Confederates to keep its arms in this tangled, Indian-infested land. Forrest had gone back on the arrangement – broken their word, plotted with the others to overcome their Yankee companions and make away with the gold, goaded either by a genuine fire to fight on for the Southern cause somehow, or by plain avarice. They were even taking young Clyman with them. The kid corporal with the roughly splinted shoulder had courage, but he was in no condition to go wandering back into the vast wilderness.

Forrest made the two newest captives sit with the others in the rock-studded shale. The wind was still whipping up spurts of dust and the first flushes of a stormy dawn were struggling through the leaden clouds. Clay Forrest's moustachioed features were painted with a faint patina of crimson as he stood amid the captives and offered his farewells. His companions were busy with the horses in the background. They were festooned with carbines and newly-filled water canteens taken from the soldiers.

'We've hitched the freshest horses to our wagon and we're takin' those in the best shape for ridin',' Forrest told the captives. 'We're also takin' the weariest horses part of the way with us. We'll leave these, some weapons an' ammunition an' a couple of canteens on the trail about a couple of miles south of here. We'll hobble the horses, but they'll probably bust loose an' wander back this way, smellin' the water. By the time you get free of your own hobbles an' make your way to the horses, we'll have had a good enough start. Some of you will have to ride double back to McDowell, of course, but you won't die of thirst an' you'll have sufficient arms to fight off any Apaches who show up.'

'That's generous of you,' retorted Travis Eade who, with Marguerite Norman, remained ungagged among the trussed-up captives.

Forrest turned his back on Eade as though the major did not exist. Young Dan Clyman came up to Eade and the girl, walking painfully and with two Spencer carbines slung from his sound shoulder.

'I just want to say thanks for the way you looked after me, Miss Norman,' he offered. 'I hope things work out well for you. There's nothin' personal in

this, it's just that I'd rather fight on where there's a
chance instead of bein' ground down by them
Yankees. You, too, Major. You did a lot for me when I
was hurt an' I appreciate it. It seems to me that
Captain Forrest is right an' I'm throwin' my hand in
with him.'

'Captain Forrest is as wrong as hell, kid,' glowered Eade. 'He's mesmerized you with crazy talk just
as he has the rest of them. When you were first
injured, he wanted to drag you all the way to Texas
before making an attempt to get some expert attention – ask the other boys. Now that you're in better
shape, thanks mostly to Captain Cowell's attention
and Miss Norman's devotion when you had fever, he
wants to take you with him on his hare-brained
move to Mexico. He's looking out for his own grasping ends and you and the rest of the boys will find it
out soon enough!'

The wind of dangerous portent was blowing out of
the widening gates of dawn with such strength that
Eade found himself shouting the final words of his
retort to the young Texan.

From beyond the rocks at the fringe of the *tinaja*,
there came the restless thump of hoofs, the tinkle of
trappings and Clay Forrest's voice calling: 'C'mon,
Clyman – we're movin' off!'

Clyman went. The sound of the departing body of
men and animals was lost in the mounting, keening
wind.

THIRTEEN

Captain Clay Forrest's delaying tactics worked to good effect.

One of the trussed-up troopers had been industriously sawing the belt which secured his wrists against the sharp edge of a half-buried rock almost from the moment he had been bound by the group of Rebels and gagged with his cavalry neckerchief. Almost twenty minutes after Forrest and his malcontents had departed, the soldier's industry brought the desired result. With his hands free, he quickly unfastened the bonds which tied his ankles together, rose, massaged his cramped bones then set about releasing Cowell, Eade and the rest of the troops.

There was a prodigious grumbling among the Yankee troopers and their opinions of the departed Southerners were voiced in lurid terms. All this time, the wind strengthened as the stormy day dawned fully. It brought stinging scarves of grit and alkali dust off the desert as it whined through the rocks and the stands of sentinel cactus around the water-sink.

Captain Cowell was enraged and he stalked the storm swept *tinaja* giving vent to his wounded feelings.

Travis Eade brought a measure of stability to the young officer.

'We're stranded on the desert, Captain,' he reminded Cowell. 'This storm is still in its early stages. It will get worse, an' Forrest and his men have left horses, weapons and water canteens out yonder. We need them and we'd better hike out there to find them. Once this storm gets its full strength, we might have a mighty hard time locating them.'

The officer and his troopers saw the wisdom of the Texan's suggestion. Some expressed doubt as to whether Forrest's party would leave the animals and the weapons, all greeted the prospect of a hike through a desert storm with the lack of enthusiasm with which any high-heeled cavalryman viewed a journey afoot, but Eade mustered half a dozen troopers under the spiky-bearded Sergeant Haggerty to accompany him on the southward trek.

They set off on a slow, plodding excursion, encumbered by their riding boots and walking with bodies bent against the sweeping wind and the furiously blown sand and alkali. Signs of the wagon's wheel tracks and the prints of the horses of Forrest's party had been cleaned by the relentless wind, but the searchers occasionally came upon sand-crusted mounds of fresh horse droppings.

The horizon was blotted out by lowering storm clouds, the wind scythed the tangled land, its blade keening oil rocks and whining across the wide-open wilderness with the wailing of dozens of lost souls and the walking men plodded onwards. Dust crusted itself into the folds of their clothing so that they appeared to be creatures carved out of the harsh substance of the land around them It stung their eyes, clogged their nostrils and its grains forced themselves between their lips to irritate their mouths.

Still they plodded, a clumsy, cursing party, all but lost in the swirling veils of blown dust. They ceased to find horse droppings and some of them concluded that they had lost the true trail taken by Forrest's band. A surly silence descended upon them, the wind mounted in its fury and Eade and Haggerty prodded the sore-footed cavalrymen onward like wranglers driving stubborn mules.

More than an hour after leaving the water-hole, they found the horses which Forrest's men had left on the desert. They blundered upon the creatures abruptly and by the sheerest chance. There were eight animals. They stood in a dejected huddle, rumps turned into the wind and heads hung low. They must have been plodding back towards the water-hole, led by the scent of the water, but the scent had been lost as the power of the wind grew. The horses had been standing stock still long enough for dust to have piled fetlock high around them and it was matted into their coats and heaped in mounds on the carbines and water canteens which Forrest and his men had slung from the saddle pommels.

The party shook the dust clear of the trappings and slung the carbines over their shoulders.

'Better lead them for a spell,' Eade suggested, 'no sense in trying to ride in this wind!' He bawled the words against the shriek of the wind, directing them at Haggerty. 'You'll have the wind at their rumps most of the way back which should make it easier for you – and the storm might blow itself out before you reach the water-hole.'

'What do you mean by *you*?' demanded Haggerty. 'You detaching yourself from us or something?' The sergeant's beard and moustache was turned tawny by encrusted dust, his eyes were screwed against the stinging flurries of grit, but they were open enough for Travis Eade to see the distinct fighting light in them.

'Don't try to obstruct me. Sergeant!' bellowed Eade. 'I'm going ahead to try to find those fools and talk some sense into them. You take your men and the rest of the horses back to the water-hole, they're needed back there.'

'You can't go ahead alone,' Haggerty protested. 'We'll come with you.'

'No!' Eade roared. 'I can handle this alone. You fellows are Yankee troopers and Forrest will whip up those men into shooting on you because of your blue coats. They won't shoot on me, I still command enough respect among them and I want those fellows to see sense and turn around for Fort McDowell. They're my men, the war's over and I don't want them to come to any harm now.'

Haggerty and his weather-punished soldiery stood around the Texas major in belligerent attitudes. Eade faced them with his jaw set at a stubbornly determined angle, one hand holding the Spencer carbine, the other clamped down on the crown of his wide hat to keep the tearing wind from snatching it from his head.

'Don't you boys try to make an effort to stop me,'

he warned. 'This is a fight that has to be worked out between Forrest and those boys and myself. According to United States' ruling, they're still rebels under arms and you could shoot at 'em. They wouldn't hesitate to shoot back. I figure I can make them see commonsense if I can catch up with them.'

'How do we know this isn't some elaborate way for you to meet up with those Johnny Rebels an' make a run south of the border with them?' Haggerty wanted to know.

'It probably is,' a young trooper opined. 'I don't trust any Johnny Rebels whoever they be. I figure we should go after 'em an' if they want to shoot it out, we'll oblige.'

Haggerty turned on the soldier swiftly. 'You ain't asked to figure anythin' out,' he reminded him, yelling through the dust-driving wind. 'I seen these fellows fight Quino's 'Paches an' they got courage runnin' out of their ears. They'll give you a fight, make no mistake about it!'

The young trooper was one of those who had ridden to the relief of the mixed party besieged at the dried out sink. He had seen only the final act of the fight against the blood-crazy desert braves and had not spent hours cooped up with the Confederates as Haggerty had. Haggerty had a big opinion of the fighting qualities of Eade and his Southerners and, having subdued the young soldier, demanded again: 'How do we know this is not just an attempt for you to join 'em an' run for Mexico, Eade?'

'Because I gave my word to Captain Cowell that I'd make my formal surrender at McDowell – and, whatever your opinion of Johnny Rebels, Sergeant, you can take it that most Confederate officers like to keep their word. And there's a second reason. My nation has been defeated in war. It's heartbreaking, but no sensible secessionist can deny that he didn't see it coming a long time ago. I saw it arriving in '63 – on the third day of a picnic we had at a place in Pennsylvania: a place they call Gettysburg!'

Eade paused for a moment and the wind took the portentous name of that Pennsylvania town and whisked it into the desert.

'When we were holed up back in that dried-out sink, the young woman told me something your president said about the end of the war. He said "We are one people now" and that started me to thinking it wasn't such a bad notion. Seems to me the South will need men who can help put the country back on its feet, men who can fight for Southern honour in peace as they did in war – and my men who're now taking off under Forrest's crazy spell are such men. I don't want them to get tangled up in any last ditch foolery.'

Eade lowered his voice as he added: 'Then, there's another thing that only Forrest and I can work out. I won't rest until I face him and settle it.'

'A personal thing?' queried Haggerty. 'The thing that made you two fight each other before Captain Cowell broke it up?'

Eade shook his head. 'That was a flash in the pan, this is something deeper. I recognized it in Forrest just before he trussed me up back at the water-hole, though I should have seen it long before. For all his fine talk about fighting on, Clay Forrest is just plain gold-greedy. He wants to get clear to Mexico with the bullion for his own sake but he wants an armed escort to help him take it through country in which Cochise might show up at any time.

'He got his escort by making fancy, patriotic talk – but he aims to see that the gold soils nobody's hands but his own. There's a real ugly streak in Captain Forrest. I saw it long ago and refused to acknowledge it. He's from Missouri and he's out of the same stable as Quantrill, Todd and Anderson!'

Travis Eade grasped the bridle of one of the horses the departing body of Southerners had left on the desert. 'It's our private fight, gentlemen, and I'll thank you to leave us to it,' he told Haggerty and his troopers. 'Tell Captain Cowell that if I don't show up at McDowell in a day or so, I'll be dead.'

He turned the horse around, yanked its head low and walked it into the teeth of the searing wind.

The California Column troopers watched him go without attempting to stop him.

FOURTEEN

Travis Eade walked the horse through the furious, grasping wind for fully an hour, his head held low and a hand clamped on the crown of his hat. It was a tortured, plodding journey in which the man was often dragging the horse by the bridle, forcing it to take one step after another over the harsh floor of the storm-torn desert. The sun gave a diffused light through the welter of blown dust, but it was hot enough to add its own measure of discomfort to Eade's battle into the teeth of the wind.

Eade had fastened the Spencer under the saddle blanket to prevent it from becoming ruined by the dust; he carried a bandolier of ammunition which had been left with the horses across his shoulders. He trudged onward with his mind a blank save for the constant, nagging urge to keep moving south and to lose as little time as possible in meeting up with Forrest's party.

An hour of this battling travail against the fury of the storm and the futility of the thing dawned on him. He had no idea of the direction in which he was travelling through the flying banners of dust. He might not be moving southwards at all. He might be blundering around in a wide circle, like a man lost in the blanket of a blizzard. Doubt assailed him. Come to consider it, suggested a devil of doubt in his ear, there was no adequate guidance to be had from the position of the sun, for the blossom of diffused brilliance beyond the obscuring curtains of dust seemed to shift its quarter with a subtle ease.

Travis Eade thought about this for a long time then became impatient with himself, muttering that the force of the storm and the welter of blowing dust must be dulling his mental processes or he would have realized long before that it was he who was moving on an erratic course and not the sun. Through the scarves of fine dust, he saw a clutter of high boulders with wind-torn yucca clumps sprouting between them. The lee of the rocks was sheltered enough to offer some comfort to both man and horse.

Eade capitulated to the storm and dragged the animal behind the boulders, pulling on the rein to bring it to its knees and shelter it more completely from the howling wind.

He sank to the earth to rest his back against one of the boulders. As he did so, his eyes and nostrils simultaneously gave him notice that his blundering quest into the storm had not been all in vain. In the sheltered lee of the boulders, undisturbed by the scything wind, there was a criss-cross of wheel marks and the mottled pockmarks of hoofprints. There were horse droppings, too, only hours old.

So they had been here. They, too, had holed up behind the boulders for a breathing spell and Eade had happened upon the place by the sheerest chance. This was too good an opportunity to lose. If he wandered out of this place and braved the restless gale again, he might well wander around for hours in an aimless zig-zag or circle. He might lose their track entirely. But if he waited here until the storm blew itself out, he might be able to strike Forrest's trail with ease – he might even see the wagon and riders on the desert when the wind dropped and the air cleared.

Eade waited, a long wait in which he fretted and fumed at the roiling storm sweeping around and above him as he huddled low behind the boulders with the patient horse.

The storm died and the tearing wind died down to a mere breeze with the rapidity of most things of the desert: nightfall, strike of angry rattler or attack of Apache. Clawing dust from his eyes and swiping it from the folds of his clothing with his hat, Travis Eade came out of the rocks. The sun was down past its noon zenith. It must be after three o'clock, the Texan imagined. Leaden clouds still scowled in a stormy roof over the land.

With his eyes clear of dust, Eade saw to his dismay how far he had wandered astray in the blanketing dust. Mountains towered in front of him, their lower slopes probably less than a dozen miles ahead.

He tried to get a grip on his scanty knowledge of the geography of this region. He recalled that when the night camp was made at the *tinaja* with Cowell and his troopers, he had noticed mountains making a brokenrimmed barrier against the sky towards the east. So he had blundered far towards the east when blanketed by the wrath of the storm, imagining that he was travelling south. He was, in fact, almost at the edge of the wasteland and entering upon country which, by the green slopes of the mountains, must be more fertile.

And yet Forrest and his crew, imagining they were heading south for Mexico, had blundered this way, too. There was evidence enough of their halt behind the sheltering rock cluster.

Eade scrunched his eyes against the still brisk and stinging breeze.

The mountains made a majestic backcloth to the bony, tumbled land. Flat-topped like all Southwestern mountains, studded with tangled outcroppings, touched by the myriad greens of spring, their deeper folds a brooding purple under the lowering thunderheads in the sky.

Then, Eade saw the betraying movement on the side of one of the rearing mountains, a tiny movement made by men and animals dwarfed almost to nothingness by the high-piled hugeness of the terrain. Eade rubbed his eyes and looked again, concentrating on the spot at which he had first noticed the slight movement. It was no illusion. They were there, angling up the side of the mountain, the wagon and the riders, following what must have been little more than an animal track.

'What made them go up there?' Travis Eade asked the breeze. 'What possible motive can Forrest have in taking the wagon up yonder? He won't get to Mexico that way!'

He went back to the horse behind the rocks, took the carbine from under the protecting blanket on the animal's back. He yanked the crumpled bandana from around his neck, carefully cleaned dust from around the breech mechanism, then slung the weapon over his shoulder. As he came out from behind the rocks, mounted and riding at an easy walk, his eyes scoured the far folds of the mountain walls. The wagon and its escort were dwarfed down to the size of mere toys up there against the rising folds of rock. They were moving along a rockface in a slow, strung-out cavalcade and they seemed to be swallowed one by one as they rode into a deep purple shadow, making a long, vertical scar down the sun-touched face. It took the closely watching rider a moment or so to conclude that the shadowed scar marked a fold in the precarious face of the mountain and Forrest and his men were following some kind of trail around it. Thus, the mountainside seemed to swallow them.

Eade prodded spurs to the hide of his mount to jerk more speed out of the weary creature.

He was off the desert and entering the fertile foothills of the mountain range, where there was an abundance of spring greenery and clumps of live-oaks, when the first blade of white lightning slashed angrily through the clouds and the first clap of thunder clattered flatly over the peaks.

And the first spattering of rain drove into his dust-crusted face on the stiff breeze.

It was raining with a steady determination, as if the elements had conspired to thoroughly drench these men who had not seen rain for weeks. The rain came in great blobs, big with the springtime bigness of buds fit to burst and hastening to meet the dry land on the powerful breeze. Texas men had been known to run around their farmyards and cavort like lambs, soaked to the skin, when this kind of rain came to break a drought.

But Clay Forrest cursed it roundly and luridly;
cursed it with a voice he tried to match against the
clashing thunder which sounded in the peaks high
over his head. The furiously driving water mocked
him. It formed on his hat and dropped down in
rivulets; it made globules on the fringe of his moustache and fell into his mouth as it articulated and
bawled forth unprintables.

As an alternative, he occasionally cursed his
fellow fugitives. They were strung out on horseback
along a ledge on which there was barely room for
two riders sitting abreast. The team pulling the
wagon had halted at a point where the trail took a
sharp twist around an outcropping of rock. The
horses had grown fractious, nervous of the thousand
foot drop which fell away at the side of the ledge.
They pawed at the surface of the rock ledge, made
slick by the pouring rain, They pawed, threw their
heads in the air with a frightened whinnying and
jingling of trappings – but they stubbornly refused
to be led around that hazardous shoulder of rock.

Forrest was at the head of the team, trying to
haul the animals around the outcropping. Thunder
growled and lightning flared to scare the horses
even more and Forrest hauled and strained, tongue-
lashing men and team.

He would never admit it, but Clay Forrest was
guilty of a large size *gaffe*. He had blundered into
the foothills of these high-rearing mountains during
the dust-storm. They had offered shelter and the
party plodded deeper into the folding land in rela-
tive comfort. Then they had spotted the upward-
winding trail. It must lead somewhere, Forrest had
argued. There were the faint cuts of many

muleshoes still to be seen in the rock. Probably it
was an old Spanish trail; possibly it led to one of the
mines the Spanish conquerors worked in the days
when this region was known as New Spain. At all
events, argued Clay Forrest, they had blundered in
the swirling dust and missed the Mexico trail, but
their blind error might yet be turned to advantage.
Sooner or later, the party at the waterhole would
raise the alarm and the California Column soldiers
from Fort McDowell would set out Mexico-wards to
look for the rebels under arms. They would never
imagine that they were in the mountains to the east.
Why not follow this old Spanish trail and hole up for
a few days until they could slip out and resume the
trip to Mexico?

The suggestion sounded reasonable enough. But
that was before the rain came to make the going
precarious, before the lightning came to frighten the
horses, before they realized how dizzily this narrow
track climbed against the side of the mountain and
before they were given this graphic demonstration
that a team of horses might not be easily persuaded
to go where nimble little pack-mules ventured.

For Clay Forrest's followers, the venture had
paled considerably. George Wain, a courageous fighting man but no mountaineer, sat rigid in his saddle,
utterly terrified to glance towards the sheer drop at
the lip of the upward spiralling trail. Mapes and
Tucker were at the rear of the wagon, hanging on to
it with one hand each to keep it forced in towards
the rising wall at their right and leading their
spooky horses with their free hands. Young Dan
Clyman, white-faced and taking little interest in the
proceedings because his injured shoulder was

jarring stabs of pain through him to send his head swimming and sicken his stomach, sat his mount towards the rear of the party. Forman rode close to him, morosely.

The rain slammed at them like wet bullets in the blustery wind.

'Should have stayed back at that water-hole,' snarled Abner Mapes bitterly. 'Major Eade was right – goin' home to the corn patch would be easier than this.'

The sentiment was shared by the others and Mapes's discontent was taken up by them. They grumbled in unison, causing Forrest, struggling with the horses' heads, to loose another broadside of profanity into the wind and rain.

'Major Eade!' he spat. 'Major Eade is a yellow, cowardly Yankee-lover. 'Specially Yankees in petticoats! He sure loves that kind!'

'*Is he, Forrest?*'

The voice came from backtrail, loud and challenging through the gusty rain.

'*If Eade is a yellow coward, let him tell you what you are. You're a common thief and several kinds of fool, Forrest. Your talk about fighting on for the Confederacy is so much hogwash. You don't intend to fight. You want this bullion for yourself, not to buy ammunition and these boys will find that out soon enough!*'

They turned and saw Travis Eade coming up the slope of the ledge towards them. He was on foot, walking at a slight crouch and he carried a Spencer carbine with its mouth downward to keep the rain from entering the muzzle. He was soaked to the skin and his mouth was drawn back into a tight grin which made his teeth show curiously white against his sun-blackened face. He kept advancing towards the party at the twist in the trail with a relentless determination.

'You fellows better get back down here, fast!' he ordered. 'Unless you have a mind to stay with Forrest in this crazy fix!'

The vertigo-stricken Wain was the first to comply. Somehow, he managed to turn his horse about and pace it slowly down the slanting ledge. Dan Clyman rode sheepishly behind him.

Travis Eade continued his progress up the rain-pelted ledge, passing the descending riders with only inches to spare at the lip of the drop.

The wagon had hidden him from Clay Forrest's view, but Forrest had ceased his struggle with the team and had hauled himself partially on to the fore of the wagon, to glower at Eade. Under the flopping, sodden brim of his hat, his face was twisted into a crazed mask of rage and he gripped his carbine menacingly.

'What d'you want, Eade?' he shouted. 'By grab, I kept my end of the bargain. I left you an' your Yankee friends horses, water an' weapons. I thought I'd seen the last of you.'

'I want to give these boys some good advice,' called Eade, still coming up the ledge in his slow, methodical way. 'I want to tell them they're fools for hitching up with you. You're looking out for yourself and you'd soon find a way of shaking these boys off once you and the gold had a safe passage to Mexico. Well, Mapes, Forman and Tucker, how do you fancy going home to the corn-patch now? Why not head back down the trail with those horses and join the other boys?'

Mapes, Tucker and Forman complied. They came down the slanting ledge-trail, gingerly, leading their horses.

Forrest was alone on the wagon, halted where the trail twisted around the shoulder of the mountain, the team shifting restlessly between the shafts. He was standing fully on the wagon now, carbine at the ready. A white stab of lightning split the sky, set the team to jumping and put a bright illumination on Forrest's face to show near crazed eyes and a hair-fringed mouth grinning in murderous anticipation.

'What're you aimin' to do, Eade?' he shouted to the advancing man.

'Nothing in particular,' shouted Travis Eade with a deceptive laziness. 'Matter of fact, I was just thinking how fitting it would be for the rest of us to just wander down to solid earth again and leave you up here with the gold you love so much. You're stranded with it. Those animals won't take another step – and you can't turn the wagon around!'

'By thunder, take another step, Eade an' I'll drop you!' yelled the infuriated Forrest.

Eade halted mere yards from the wagon and shook his head slowly.

'Sure is funny, Forrest. You schemed for that gold and now you've got it. Your companions have seen the light and you can't do a blamed thing with just the bullion and you and the horses to share this ledge.'

Through the rain, Forrest shouted, with a hysterical jaggedness to his voice: 'Of course I schemed for it. I made up my mind that if ever I got clear of that dried-up sink, I'd have the gold. D'you figure I fought in the war for nothin' but to go back to

Missouri to live in poverty under Yankee rule? If
there was any loot goin' to anyone out of this war, I
aimed to make sure it didn't all go to the Yankees!'

All the Missouri Border Ruffian in Forrest was on
the surface now. His rain-streaked face was
contorted with a near-insane rage as he shrieked
through the wind-driven downpour: 'By thunder,
Eade, I got this far with the gold an' I won't be
stopped by you!'

Forrest's eyes were flaring with a light of hatred
and the carbine was suddenly clamped up to his
shoulder. Travis Eade hurled himself down to the
rain-slicked ledge a split second before he fired.

The carbine slammed a hollow, bellowing report
through the mountains, its slug drove against the
rock wall over the Texas major's head and whanged
off it with a high-pitched scream. From his prone
position, Eade looked up as he heard the frightened
screech of horses, the jangle of trappings and a wild,
hoarse scream climbing above these sounds.

Through a curtain of rain which imparted a dim,
dream-like appearance to the drama, he saw the
horses and wagon outlined against the lip of the
ledge, the animals, already frightened by their
precarious position, bucking high into nothingness
at the close-confined blast of the carbine – plunging
over the edge and taking the wagon and Forrest
with them. For a brief instant, he saw Clay Forrest
spreadeagled in thin air, still gripping the carbine.
Then, horses, wagon and man were gone, obliterated
in a tremendous storm of falling rock and dirt which
was showering down the rock face and pouring off
into the gulf into which the wagon had fallen.

Eade sprawled flat on the wet rock of the ledge as

it shook under the impact of tons of tumbling rock, smiting the trail a little way ahead of him. He inched back down the slope of the trail, making as fast a retreat as he could on his stomach.

Forrest's blasting carbine, slamming against the rock wall, had sent its clamour awakening echoes – and had dislodged loose rock and earth which might have been poised above this ledge-trail for centuries. It thundered down in a brief but furious cascade.

For a long time, Travis Eade made his backward crawling journey down the slope. When he looked up again, the avalanche had ceased and a thin fog of dust mingled with the rain at the point where the wagon had pitched over the lip. Slowly, Eade stood up and ventured to the rim of the ledge to look down. There was a thousand foot drop and, at the bottom of the cleft, a pall of dust hung over a heap of newly tumbled boulders and earth. Clay Forrest, the horses, the wagon and the Confederate gold were totally buried.

Eade walked down the precarious ledge slowly and sick at the stomach. Ahead of him, he saw Mapes, Clyman, Tucker, Forman and Wain, progressing slowly downwards on horseback, not daring to look back.

He heard the sound of his horse, tethered at the foot of the ledge-trail, whinnying as it sensed the approach of the other horses. There was a welcome in the sound, just as there was a welcome in the sight of the wide land below. Fort McDowell was down there, somewhere beyond those tumbled, wasteland miles. It would be good to arrive there and rest. It would be good to see Marguerite Norman again.

The rain slackened and stopped and the sun came from behind the last of the storm clouds, bright and promising.